Legacy and the Queen

LEGACY
AND THE
QUEEN

CREATED BY

KOBE
BRYANT

WRITTEN BY

ANNIE
MATTHEW

GRANITY STUDIOS
COSTA MESA, CALIFORNIA

*To Nani, Gigi, B.B., and KoKo, my four
beautiful, spirited, strong daughters:
When you fiercely protect your passion,
no one can ever steal your dreams.*
—Kobe Bryant

To David and Sammy
—Annie Matthew

CHAPTER ONE

THE LIGHT OF THE MOON

O n the morning of her twelfth birthday, Legacy Petrin woke from a dream about playing tennis with a winged racket.

She was smiling when she blinked awake. For a few moments, she let herself focus on the tawny lines of the stain on the ceiling. The webbed shape had been spreading for years, the result of water damage from a storm that had raged through the countryside before she could remember. Now the stain was almost comforting, like the unfolding map of a secret magical city.

Only once her eyes reached the edge of her secret city did the uncomfortable thoughts start flooding her mind. She remembered how funding for the orphanage had been cut. She remembered the new white strands in her father's close-cropped hair and how his hands had trembled when he lit the lamps after dinner last night.

By the time Legacy sat up in bed, her worries had formed a knot in her throat. When she swung her legs over the edge of the mattress, the tumbled stones of the floor pressed their cold fists into her arches. Shivering, she reached under the bed and pulled out her racket.

The wood frame was warped, and the old strings were fraying.

The bark grip was now nearly black, imprinted with the shape of her palm. But Legacy loved that racket more than any object she'd ever possessed. Holding it, she felt like herself. A new sense of calm spread through her body.

When she stood and crossed the room, carrying her racket and a balding tennis ball, the stones underfoot were no longer so cold. Trying not to make any noise, she passed the long row of beds where the littles were sleeping. She paused only to kiss Ink on the forehead.

In sleep, Ink's face was angelic: soft brown, dimpled, and surrounded by a halo of sun-kissed curls. With both of her little hands, she was clutching her beloved blanket.

It was the same blanket she'd been fearfully gripping when, not even a year ago, Legacy found her abandoned on the stone steps of the orphanage.

Back then, Ink had been too frightened to talk. She'd been too frightened to sleep. Now Ink was braver. Legacy had taught her to wear her blanket as a cape. And whenever she did, she became a new little girl: bossy and bold, capable of ordering the older littles to take parts they didn't want in the elaborate plays she directed.

Smiling to herself, Legacy moved on toward the door. She only paused again before the last bed, where Van—Legacy's best friend, and the only kid at the orphanage who was her age—was still sleeping as well. His head was always hot when he slept: there was a light sheen of sweat on his forehead. His skin was the color of wet cycapress bark. The colossal book he'd been reading—Eleander's *Novica: A History, Scientific and Otherwise, of the Republic of Nova*—was splayed over his skinny chest, and his mouth was open, a silver thread of drool trailing out of the corner and down his chin. He'd forgotten to take off his glasses. They rested crookedly over the bridge of his nose.

Legacy smiled. While he was still sleeping, at least, his face was peaceful. He hadn't yet picked up his daily delivery of the *Nova Times*. His eyes hadn't yet darkened in indignation, and he hadn't yet begun to rant about the historical reasons for poverty in the provinces or the lingering effects of the Great Fire, despite all of High Consul Silla's reforms.

For now, he was only occupied with his dreams. And that was how it should be, Legacy thought as she slipped down the back stairs and out through the kitchen.

She sat down on the stone steps that led to the garden and laced up her sneakers. Outside, it was still dark. Surrounded on one side by dusky olive trees of the agricultural valley, and on the other side by the slope leading up to the Forest of Cora, the garden seemed to sit in a big bowl of silence. Only occasionally was that silence broken by a faint boom from deep in the mines, somewhere beyond the agricultural district, Agricio. The vibrations spread through the earth and crept up through Legacy's sneakers, stirring memories of the articles Van liked to read over breakfast, about dangerous mining conditions and pollution in the provinces.

For a moment, the knot formed again in Legacy's throat. But as soon as she was hitting the ball against the stone wall of the garden, the last of her worries slipped away. She was alone. Not even the birds were awake. There were no chores to be done, no little faces to wash, no small socks to wrestle onto wriggling feet. For now, all Legacy had to do was play tennis.

She started with ground strokes. The morning was cool, but while she moved, her body grew warmer. The only steady sound was the *plonk* of the tennis ball bouncing on stone and the *ping* of the ball striking her strings. In the darkness, Legacy could barely make out the ball as it bounced off the rough stones of the wall, spewing off in unpredictable trajectories, as though she were playing an extraordinarily skillful opponent. Sometimes, the ball got lost in shadow, and she had to search for it in the weeds choking the garden or in the roots of the cycapress trees.

But once she'd settled into her rhythm, her eyes began to adjust. The pale light of the moon began to seem brighter. Legacy found that she could make out every crack and divot in the rough stone of the wall. She could anticipate the ball's angle. She moved into her shots, taking them faster and faster, swinging hard over the top of the ball so that the sound it made when it struck her strings was cleaner.

Then she began to aim for the same stone in the wall. Then she forced herself to aim for the same divot in the same stone. Time and time again, she hit her mark. She poured her whole weight into each shot. Certainty spread through every muscle in her body.

When she finished that drill, she moved up to the wall, practicing volleys. Between shots, she felt a smile creeping over her face. She was so lucky, she thought. Even if they were down a goat since the day before yesterday, when the new kid wandered into the forest. Even if now they barely had enough milk for the littles. Even if she'd been hungry for days.

Even so, she had her racket. She had the wall to play against in the mornings.

Maybe she wasn't as good as Gia, the top tennis player in Nova, who attacked her ground strokes with a long, honey-blond braid swinging behind her and those thick stripes of black paint under her eyes. In

4

Van's copy of the *Nova Times*, Legacy had read all the stories about how Gia's grana was growing stronger every day. About how she could make the sky turn dark over her opponents, how she could cause the shadows to lengthen so that it was difficult for her opponents to keep the ball.

But that didn't matter to Legacy now. All that mattered was the feel of the ball striking her strings, and the certainty in her own body.

Or at least that's what she was thinking when the sound of something stumbling around in the garden startled her and caused her to lose track of the ball.

"How are you doing that?" Van called out through the darkness.

Legacy breathed a sigh of relief. For a moment, she'd allowed herself to imagine one of those monsters from the Cora stories. A giant crackle, maybe. Or a lural with ice-blue eyes and sickle-shaped fangs.

"Seriously, bud," Van was saying. He must have finished taking care of the goats. Now he was moving toward her, feeling his way through the darkness, until he tripped over a root, caught himself, ran a hand over his hair, then propped himself casually against the trunk of a cyca-press tree.

Legacy focused on the strings of her racket, acting as if she hadn't seen his near miss. He was always so self-conscious about his clumsiness, Legacy thought. Then she tried to swallow the little surge of guilt that had crawled up from her stomach.

"Where was that light coming from?" Van said.

"What light?" Legacy said.

"The light you're using to see the ball," Van said.

Legacy looked around, then shrugged. "The sun's rising," she said. Though now that she'd stopped playing, it did seem darker than it had before.

5

"I can't see a thing," Van said. "And you're getting every shot! It must be some kind of grana."

"Or it's getting light out," Legacy said.

"I'm telling you, bud," Van said, "you have all the grana you need. All you need now is a better racket and a little serious training—which is why this is such incredible news!"

Now he was waving his copy of the *Nova Times* over his head. His glasses had gone crooked again. No matter how many times Legacy tried to fix them, they never quite balanced on the bridge of his nose.

"What are you talking about?" Legacy said, peering at the newspaper.

"I'm talking about change," Van said. "I'm talking about progress!"

"What are you actually talking about," Legacy said, rolling her eyes.

"The Queen," Van said, "has announced that she's holding a free trial for children from the provinces."

Legacy peered over his shoulder. High Consul Silla—otherwise known as the Queen, since her younger days on the tennis court, when she dominated her opponents so thoroughly she seemed to wear an invisible crown on her head—must have announced a new provincial outreach program.

"Winner gets a free ride to the academy," Van said. "And a slot in the qualifiers for the national championships!"

For a moment, Legacy's heart seemed to have sprouted wings. Now they were flapping wildly against the cage of her chest. How many nights had she gone to sleep dreaming of training at Silla's academy? How many times had she closed her eyes and seen herself playing the national championships?

She'd even imagined winning them, beating Gia, the best player in the republic, and kneeling to pledge her loyalty to High Consul Silla,

6

who would stand before her with that regal composure that was the source of her nickname and that made her so beloved by the people of Nova.

Legacy had dreamed of that moment while teaching the littles to read. She'd dreamed of it while preparing their bottles. Hanging their wet pajamas up on the line in the garden, she'd closed her eyes and heard the applause of all the citizens who had come to watch her play in the finals. She'd felt the grass of the academy courts giving under her feet. She'd imagined herself changing the weather like the other top players. Like Villy Sal, who could cause snow to swirl down on his opponents. Or Sondra Domenicu, who could make the ground of the court start to shudder and crack. Legacy had imagined beating them all.

But now, hearing Van say it out loud, Legacy shook her head as if to clear out all the fantasies. It was one thing to have daydreams while washing the littles' pajamas. But it was another thing entirely to let herself believe they were real.

Even if she did win the trials, she couldn't run off to train at the academy. She had responsibilities here. How would her father manage without her? Ever since her mother left, it had been the two of them. As soon as she was old enough, she'd tried to do whatever she could to help him run the orphanage. But she'd seen how the responsibility had worn him down. She'd watched the lines in his face grow deeper. She'd watched the white crawl into his close-cropped hair.

And anyway: he'd already been abandoned once. Legacy wouldn't let it happen again. Especially not so that she could follow some silly dream about tennis.

But Van was still at it. "Are you listening?" he said, following close behind while Legacy moved around the garden, beating clumps of

7

weeds with her racket, looking for the lost ball. If her father found it in the garden, he'd know she'd been playing tennis. Then she'd get another one of his lectures.

"You'll win those trials, I know it!" Van said. "And then you'll go to the academy. And once you've gotten some quality coaching, you'll win the nationals, too. And with the money you make there, you can fix all the problems at the orphanage."

Legacy found the ball under a broken flowerpot. She trapped it against the side of her sneaker, balanced it on her racket, and headed toward the kitchen stairs.

Behind her, Van was still yammering on. "It's perfect timing. It's meant to be. The trials are tomorrow. And today's your birthday, so you'll finally get that Tempest. Then you'll have more power, and you'll be able to express grana. You can use it when you're playing the trials!"

On the stairs, Legacy picked up her pace. She hoped Van couldn't see her face flush. For months, he'd been after her about asking for a Tempest for her twelfth birthday. It was all part of his master plan to make her into the greatest champion in the republic. Never mind the fact that she'd never even had a coach. Never mind that players like Gia had been training at the academy since they could walk, learning how to express grana that Legacy couldn't so much as dream of. Never mind that a single day at the academy cost more than the orphanage budget for a whole month.

None of that made any difference to Van. He was sure that Legacy could win the nationals and save the orphanage. Then maybe he could go to the School of Economics and become a historian, and later a politician, or even a senator who could aid Silla in her reform of the republic.

Legacy didn't interrupt him while he rambled on. She knew that his

8

schemes distracted him from his hunger and from the occasional pains in his bad leg. They prevented him from thinking about what he'd do when he was too old to keep his bed at the orphanage and there wasn't money to send him to college.

Usually, Van's hopeful chatter made Legacy happy. But now, listening while Van rattled off stats about how much a Tempest would help the accuracy of her serve, Legacy felt her face growing redder.

She wasn't going to get that Tempest.

She hadn't even asked for it.

She'd considered it, but in the end it seemed selfish. How could she justify asking for a new racket when the littles didn't even have enough milk for their bottles? Instead, she'd asked for a book of Cora stories for Ink. She'd been excited to see Ink turn them into plays. But she hadn't considered how disappointed Van would be when she didn't get that Tempest.

Legacy paused at the kitchen door. Beyond the garden wall, the sun was actually rising now. For the most part, the slopes and valleys of Agricio had recovered since the Great Fire that was still raging through them three years ago. Since Silla put it out, money had been set aside by the senate for new olive trees to replace the ones that had burned. Stripes of silver-green saplings trained to their stakes stretched off down into the valley, where blue clouds had nestled in for the night and still hadn't risen with the morning.

On the other side of the garden, however, the Forest of Cora was ravaged. The first waves of recovery money hadn't been sent there. And now that the recovery had racked up staggering debts, Legacy couldn't imagine funds would be sent anytime soon.

The skeletons of the burnt drammus trees stood black against the rosy

9

sky. They seemed to be wagging their skinny, leafless fingers at her, reminding her that it was absurd to dream of winning those trials. Her only responsible option, those trees seemed to say, was to remain at the orphanage.

Sighing in resignation, Legacy headed inside. Her father must have started the kitchen fire without her. And in the great room, the littles were already assembled at the long wooden table.

"Happy birthday!" they all cried in unison when Legacy stepped into the room.

Legacy smiled. They must have all chipped in to set the table and lay out the corn cakes. They'd even made an effort to dress themselves so she wouldn't have to. Ink's burlap shift was on backward. Leo's sneakers were on the wrong feet. And it must have been Hugo who combed Zaza's slippery, tangle-prone hair.

But they all looked so proud of the effort. Someone had even found a hunk of wild honey and placed it at the center of the table for Legacy to spread on her corn cake. Seeing that, Legacy smiled wider. So many wild bees had died in the fire. Now the fruits of their labor were rare. It had been months since anyone had found wild honey.

Anticipating the sweet, warm taste of the honey, Legacy sat down at the place they'd set for her. Beside her plate was a large rectangular box wrapped in brown paper.

Before she opened it, she glanced up at her father. He was sitting quietly at the head of the table. There was that white in his hair, and his shoulders were a little more stooped than usual. But when he smiled, Legacy could almost remember how he looked when her mother hadn't yet left.

He used to play with her in the garden. He'd thrown tennis balls for her to chase, and she'd laughed and laughed while she retrieved them.

Now Legacy looked back at the box on the table.

"Open it!" Van urged, standing beside her with a goofy grin.

Once again, Legacy flushed. She hesitated. But there was nothing she could do now. She opened the package and drew out the heavy book.

Ink let out a squeal. "Cora stories!" she cried, lifting her cape in excitement. "We'll start a new play this afternoon!"

When Legacy finally faced Van, she saw that his face had crumpled like a used napkin. His glasses had gone crooked again. This time he didn't make the effort to fix them.

"Did you even ask?" he said. "Did you even *ask* for the racket?"

Legacy tried to swallow the stone in her throat. It wouldn't go down. She couldn't answer.

"You won't go, will you?" Van said. Tears were welling at the corners of his eyes. "You won't even *try*."

"Van," Legacy started, but he was already running off toward the staircase. He moved as quickly as he could, but his bad leg was slowing him down, and he must have been blinded by his tears, because he tripped on the first stair, and again on the second, and this time he didn't try to make it seem graceful. He only pulled himself up and kept running.

CHAPTER TWO

THE FOREST
OF CORA

After breakfast, Legacy spent a few hours entertaining the littles. They gathered around her, sitting cross-legged on the tumbled stone floor, and Legacy read to them from the book of Cora stories.

It was a bit battered by time, its corners softened and its pages yellowing at the edges. It would have been impossible for her father to find a new copy, because newer copies didn't exist. Under Silla, in the months after the Great Fire had been put out, the senate had banned worship of the old gods. Too many acts of destruction had been perpetrated in their names.

But enforcement was not as strict in the provinces as it was in the city, and there were ways to find old books and relics. And what harm could there be, Legacy thought, in reading some stories to keep the littles distracted? It wasn't as if she were invoking the gods to use their powers. She wasn't asking the gods to alter the weather. She was only describing their adventures for the entertainment of the littles.

The old book was as heavy as an armload of bricks. And though the pages were dusty and torn, the illustrations were painted with luminous mineral pigments: gold, aquamarine, vermilion, and pink. Most of the stories were set in the Forest of Cora. It was unburned then, and the trees in the pictures—nipperberries and cycapresses, but most of all the glorious drammus trees that used to be the pride of the forest—were verdant and teeming with life, nothing like the burnt husks that now lined the hillsides. The trunks of the drammus trees were gargantuan, composed sometimes of six or seven trunks braided together, and their branches cascaded down, trailing leaves like shredded green banners.

In the pictures of the forest, you could see the occasional pyrus, one of Cora's winged horses. They were furry and gray, with white markings, gentle eyes, and enormous pink wings. There were also illustrations of the lurals that stalked the forest undergrowth, savage animals with the spotted coats of leopards and the blue eyes and sickled fangs of wolves.

Sometimes, the pictures showed lurals leaping toward pyruses, who reared away, breathing fire as they did when threatened.

At the ends of the stories, in complicated calligraphy, there were always strange, inexplicable morals, their lettering illuminated in gold: phrases like

Anger fed is quickly dead

A self disguised is a death surmised

A dream come to life is the end of all strife

Legacy didn't always understand these morals, and she imagined the littles didn't, either, but they liked the sounds of the words. They liked the big, brilliant pictures. Before long, Ink was rushing around in her cape, ordering the older littles to take their places onstage.

"You're Metus, the god of fear!" Ink was saying to Leo when Legacy finally stood and headed off to the stairs. "And I'm Cora, the goddess of love!"

"Why am I always fear?" Leo grumbled, and Legacy started to smile. But then she remembered Van's face when she hadn't pulled out the Tempest. She remembered the way he'd tripped on the stairs.

She hoped he'd found his way to the attic. That was where he went to read about the history of the republic in dusty old volumes, snacking on the bits of stale corn cake he was always pulling out of his pockets. He liked to sit in a nest of old, moth-eaten tapestries, dropping crumbs on the tasseled silk pillows.

All the dusty artifacts in the attic were relics of the days when the orphanage had been a country estate. Now the tapestries—once displayed on the walls—had been wound into thick bolts. The throw pillows were discolored by mildew, and the books were warped and water stained. But the attic was still Van's favorite place in the orphanage. He spent hours up there every day, reading about the old ways: the noble senators who ruled in the peaceful years before the civil war and the tennis champions who came to the city from the provinces and pledged their loyalty to whichever senator most inspired their trust.

As she climbed the stairs, Legacy assumed Van had taken refuge in a dusty tome, so she was surprised when she ran into him in the hallway instead. He was standing outside her father's bedroom.

When she approached, he put a finger to his lips. He gestured to the crack in the door.

Legacy took a step forward. Through the crack, she could see a stripe of her father. He seemed to be kneeling before a small table that Legacy had never seen. On top of it, there was a figurine, a woman who herself was prostrate in front of a pyrus, her forehead resting on the ground.

"Dear Cora," her father was saying. "Please guide me."

Legacy's mouth dropped open. Was this what a prayer looked like? She'd never seen her father pray. She'd never seen anyone pray, outside of the old books. Prayer, for one thing, was illegal. And her father had always been a believer in balance and reason. The gods were invoked in moments of strong feeling or passion. How could her father be calling to Cora?

"Help me, Cora," he was saying, "to have the strength to send him to work."

"Him?" Legacy whispered to Van, but Van lifted his finger again.

"Help me," her father said, "to know that by sacrificing one, I'll be able to look after the others."

Legacy leaned in closer to the crack. She didn't like this at all. Who did her father plan to send to work? And why was he *praying* about it? He looked so small, so vulnerable, bent on his knees. He looked almost like a child, as though his adulthood had only been a costume, one that he'd now shed, becoming as helpless as one of the littles.

"And please," her father said, "help Van to know that I love him."

Van? Legacy thought. *Van?*

Her face was growing hot. Her father wanted to send *Van* to work?

15

But where could he go? He had no education that would be recognized in the city. And what could he do in the provinces, with his limp and his glasses and his skinny arms? He was the smartest kid Legacy had ever met, but he wasn't the strongest. He could barely manage carrying full pails of milk in from the barn, let alone long days of harvesting olives.

"Help me," her father was saying, "to have faith that he'll survive the factories. And that he'll understand the decision I've made."

A fist clenched in Legacy's stomach. The *factories*? Van would never survive it. She'd heard stories of ten-hour shifts, kids not much older than her hauling loads of mineral compounds shipped in from the mines. Pumping the bellows for hours on end, heating the metal until it could be drawn into threads.

When would Van read? How would he finish his education? How could her father imagine Van was suited to that kind of work?

Legacy glanced over her shoulder at Van. Had he known about this scheme? Was that why he wanted her to go play the trials? Now, in the hallway, his face was ashen, but he didn't speak. She saw again how frail his shoulders were.

Then she remembered that other day. His shoulders had looked frail then, as well, when he was pinned under that branch, struggling to get out. With a rush of shame, Legacy remembered the blinding flash of light and the way the branch had fallen. She'd tried to pull Van out by his shoulders, but she couldn't manage it until her father came running.

Before Legacy knew what she was doing, she was charging through her father's door.

"You can't send him," she said. "It's not right."

Her father pulled himself up. His face had darkened with anger, and suddenly Legacy realized that he was not, in fact, as vulnerable as a child.

16

And she'd just revealed that she'd been eavesdropping at his door. And on top of that, she'd rushed into his room without his permission.

Looking up at her father's darkening face, Legacy considered running away. But then, once again, she remembered the day that branch fell and pinned Van.

"Don't send him," she said. "Send me instead."

Legacy saw the clench of her father's jaw.

"You're not old enough," he said.

"He's only a year older than I am," Legacy said.

"I need your help here," her father said.

Legacy's nails dug into her palms. "Then let me go to Silla's trials," she said. "Let me try to win. If I do, I can train at the academy. I can start winning money, and I'll send it back and—"

"Legacy!" her father said. "Listen to yourself. You're talking about fantasies. You're talking about dreams. But this is the real world that we live in. There's real work to be done. How would I manage the orphanage without you?"

Legacy stared up at him. How could she explain to him how it felt when she played tennis on the back wall? How could she make him understand that playing tennis was the one thing she was made for, that it wasn't just a dream, that it was the realest of her realities?

"I could do it," she tried, but she felt her confidence failing. "I could—"

But her father was already shaking his head. "How could you, Legacy? How could you choose this moment to bring up the old argument about tennis?"

Legacy tried to summon a defense and found that she couldn't.

"You can't just think about yourself," her father said. "Think about

17

the littles. There are other people you have to consider."

Now, no matter how hard Legacy clenched her fists, the tears started to fall. "Please," she said. "Just let me tr—"

"So stubborn!" her father said. His eyes had gone cold. "Just like your mother."

A sob ripped through Legacy's chest. Then she was running away. She passed Van in the hallway, stumbled down the stone stairs, and must have let herself out through the gate, because she was running up the slope to the Forest of Cora, where she pushed her way past the scratching fingers of the burnt trees, heading deeper into the gloom beneath their dead branches.

———————

Once her lungs started burning, Legacy slowed to a walk. Then she looked around. She had never ventured this far into the forest. There were other kinds of trees here, not just the burnt drammus trees that crowded the edges. The trunks of the drammus trees seemed to be made of charcoal: satiny black and evenly quilted. All of them had been killed in the fire. But some of the other trees seemed to have withstood the worst flames. Here, deeper in the forest, Legacy found a few nipper-berry trees that were still bearing fruit. There were other trees too, trees that Legacy didn't recognize. Some of them had grown leaves since the fire, and their canopies had twisted together until they blocked out the afternoon sunlight. The darkness hung around Legacy's shoulders like velvet. These trees, the ones she didn't recognize, seemed wild and unruly. Their trunks were whorled and knotted, their leaves a disorganized jumble of shapes: mittens, goldfish, unfurled umbrellas.

She realized it had been a long time since she'd heard birdsong.

She couldn't hear the explosions deep in the mines, either, or feel their vibrations in the soles of her sneakers. In fact, she could feel nothing but the soft moss underfoot. Its cushiony thickness absorbed the sounds of her footsteps, though sometimes, when she stepped on a burnt branch, she could hear a faint whisper as it disintegrated, giving way to a sigh of black dust.

Everything was so quiet. Legacy wondered if she shouted—if she screamed for help—whether anyone in the world would be able to hear her.

Her heart beat faster as her eyes adjusted to the darkness. Disturbing new details began to emerge from the gloom. If she looked too long at the whorled trunks, she saw the shapes of unhappy faces etched into their bark: women with long, snarled hair; men with skin sagging loose on their faces.

As her ears got used to the new silence, she began to make out sounds that she hadn't noticed: branches clicking like fingernails on a window, small animals skittering over tangled roots. Then a large shape rushed screeching toward her head, only veering away at the last moment with a great crashing through the canopy.

Spooked, Legacy tried to steady herself by grabbing a low-hanging branch. But she only managed to break off a burnt twig, and then her heart froze in her chest when she heard a moan of pain from the branch she'd just broken.

She looked down at her hand. A drop of blood gleamed on the twig she was holding.

For a moment, Legacy stood rooted to the spot. Was it her hand or the twig that was bleeding? When she looked up again, the tree was bending toward her: a tall, treacherous form leaning down to enclose her. Recoiling in horror, she shook free and ran until she emerged into a clearing.

There, Legacy stopped. She took a step forward. Her jaw dropped. The clearing looked almost like a tennis court.

It was wild and overgrown, but still: it had the rectangular shape of a court. There, almost obscured by the overgrown grass, were faded white lines. And there, at the center, was a sagging black net.

Legacy took another step forward. What *was* this place? Who could have built a court so deep in this forest?

More questions bloomed in Legacy's mind as she walked the length of the court, following its alley line. Who had played here? Who had maintained it so far away from the city? Mowing it, painting its lines, tending it every day until one day he—or she—stopped?

At the drooping net, Legacy paused. Her eyes were drawn to the place where a referee chair would have stood, in pictures she'd seen of the academy courts. In its place, however, there was a gargantuan tree. Its trunk seemed to be built of five thick, braided strands. Its branches drooped down, swaying gently in the breeze. And its leaves—though spare and somewhat tattered—hung from its branches like shredded green banners.

Stunned, Legacy walked across the court. All the drammus trees were said to have burned. They'd gone extinct in the fire. There wasn't a living one left in the republic.

And yet, there it was. She could hear the whispering of its long, graceful branches swaying slightly in the breeze. It almost sounded as if they were speaking to her softly, beckoning her to come closer.

At the base of the tree, she found a place to sit among the thick, knotted roots. Then she closed her eyes and breathed in. That scent—she was sure she remembered it. It was sweet, like honey, and green as grass. It made her heart grow warm in her chest. She'd almost placed it when one of the branches brushed her cheek.

Its leaves were soft as the finest silk. And the whispering of its branches almost sounded like those strange morals from the book of stories: *Anger fed is quickly dead. A dream come to life is the end of all strife.*

Then, keeping her eyes closed, listening to that whispering voice, feeling the gentle touch of those leaves, Legacy heard her mother.

"Go," her mother whispered. "Go to the trials."

Legacy's eyes startled open. She looked around. And already, tears were starting to prick.

Because of course it hadn't been her mother's voice.

Her mother hadn't come back. Legacy was alone in the clearing.

But it was her mother's scent she was smelling. She knew that as surely as she knew that she was alone. That was her mother's scent, from back in those days in the garden, when they'd all played together, laughing and hugging one another.

For several more hours, Legacy remained by the side of the old court, under the canopy of the drammus. It was hard for her to pull herself away. By the time she finally made her way out to the edge of the forest, it was already evening.

In the garden, the cycapress trees twisted into the sky like daggers. The kitchen was full of hulking dark shapes.

When Legacy climbed the stairs to the attic, she found Van in one of his nests. He was eating a corn cake and reading a thick book entitled *Metium Mining Mechanics.*

For a moment, before he looked up, Legacy watched him. His nose was buried deep in his book on mechanics, but she saw that the book on his lap was deep green. Its cover was made of thick cloth, with an embroidered gold leaf at the center.

"A drammus leaf," she said, pointing to the green book, but Van gave her an odd look.

"Where?" he said, glancing down. He picked up the green book and flipped through a few pages. His brow was furrowed in confusion. "It's just a blank book," he said.

Legacy stared at him. Even from across the attic, she could see writing on the pages. But before she could protest, Van had closed the book and stood up.

"Bud," he said. "I'm sorry. I know you can't go. I just—"

"No," Legacy said, cutting him short. "I'm going."

Van blinked at her through his crooked glasses.

"Tomorrow," Legacy said. "I'm going to play in those trials."

CHAPTER THREE

FURNACE
FLAMES

It was still dark when Legacy snuck out of the orphanage carrying nothing but her racket, an extra roll of bark grip, and a few corn cakes stuffed into a flour sack.

On her way out, she kissed each of the littles. Van had promised to be gentle when he combed Zaza's hair and to listen when Leo woke from one of his nightmares. She'd drilled him on which stories to read to them before bed and how to wash pots without scratching the surface.

But even so, when she closed the door to their bedroom, it was difficult for her to swallow her guilt. As she made her way down the hall, she paused in front of her father's door. She and Van had weighed a thousand ways for her to tell him she was leaving, but they both knew that no matter what she said, he wouldn't let her walk out the door. So Legacy didn't say goodbye. She passed his bedroom and snuck out the front door.

Walking down the long driveway, it was hard for her to shake the idea that maybe this was how her mother had felt on the day she left. Maybe she, too, felt her stomach tie itself into knots, thinking about how her father would feel when he realized she'd abandoned him.

Realizing that, Legacy almost turned and ran back. But just then she heard the wheels of a cart approaching the driveway, and then she was running behind it. She'd heard of other provi kids catching cart rides into the city and never imagined that she, too, would take a deep breath, squeeze her eyes shut, and leap onto the hay-scattered bed. She found a seat between a few cages of chickens.

Noticing her intrusion, the chickens began squawking and indignantly flapping their wings, their eyes bulging out of their faces. After a few moments, they settled down, but in the darkness, she could still see the whites of the chickens' eyes. They seemed to be watching her nervously, as if assessing whether or not she was a threat.

She wished that she could comfort them. Or open their cages and let them all out before they became some city dweller's dinner. But she didn't dare lose her ride, so she settled on humming one of the songs she sometimes sang to the littles, until finally the chickens seemed to calm down.

By then, they'd left Agricio. It was so much smaller, really, than Legacy had imagined. Somehow, her whole life, she'd believed that those hillsides covered with olive trees must stretch on forever. Van had told her that she'd leave them behind and move through the mining district, Minori, on her way to the trials, which would be held just outside the city gates. But she hadn't thought she'd leave the landscape of her childhood behind her so quickly. Already, off in the distance, Legacy could make out the fires from smokestacks in the factories.

On clear days, you could see them from the orphanage. And she'd seen pictures in the *Nova Times*, describing the declining conditions of the mines and the refineries. They'd been damaged in the Great Fire, and despite Silla's efforts, they'd never been fully repaired. Still, as the cart came closer, Legacy could smell oily smoke pouring out of the smokestacks. She saw flames leaping from the furnaces.

Now, in their reddish light, Legacy could see the enormous, rust-red gashes of metium mines in the distance. She could see the glittering gray craters of the prosite mines. Carts heaped with ore crawled out of the cavities. And beyond them, factories heaved up into the sky: dark, ugly buildings with chimneys belching black smoke.

Legacy shivered. She felt tiny and powerless before the colossal structures rising before her. In every direction around the factories, scrap-metal shacks sprawled into the distance. Van had shown her a picture of these and explained to Legacy that they were built by workers who came from other provinces in the wake of the Great Fire. Even when production in the other provinces had shut down, the mines and the refineries remained open, so workers had flooded in. Some left their families behind, abandoning them at places like the orphanage. Some brought their children along. Even now, three years since Silla managed to extinguish the fire, it almost seemed to Legacy as if half the country must live in those ramshackle scrap-metal cities.

Those, Legacy realized, were the shacks where Van would live if he went to work in the factories. Imagining him there—with no books to read and no old tapestries to curl up on—Legacy felt a cold hard claw curl in her stomach. She tried to distract herself by opening her flour sack and inspecting the possessions she'd brought. She rummaged around for the corn cakes, her racket, the extra roll of bark grip, and was surprised when her hand hit something solid and rectangular that she hadn't placed there.

She pulled it out. It was the green book Van had been holding; he must have snuck it into her sack. She picked it up and opened it, and a little note fluttered out, landing in the hay by Legacy's sneaker.

Just thought this might be meant for you. Think of me when you're famous! From. Van

Legacy smiled and tucked the note back into the book. Then she examined its woven cover, embroidered with a gold drammus leaf. The title was sewn in gold thread:

THE BOOK OF MUSE

And on the first page, there was a stitched note:

for Legacy, from Amata

Legacy stared. Who was Amata? And why had she given Legacy a needlepoint book?

Flipping through the book's pages, Legacy saw all kinds of intricate little figures stitched in bright thread: A gray pyrus with silky pink wings. A multicolored cat. A row of jewel-colored tinctures.

They were all so vivid: How could Van have called it an empty old book? It was true that some of the colors had faded. Some of the pages seemed to have come partly unstitched, and in a few spots, the thread was worn bare.

But even so, most of the pages were full. Some of them seemed to contain what looked to Legacy like recipes for very bad dinners. Others contained lists of strange mineral compounds, a "diagram for proper pyrus mount," and a "chant for avoiding scorched eyebrows."

But none of them answered Legacy's questions. Why had this "Amata" given her a book of recipes and chants? And why had it been stashed away in the attic?

By the time Legacy finally looked up from the book, the sun had risen. The sky was watery, shot through with tentacles of bright color, and she could see the city off in the distance. A wall encircled the perimeter. Above it rose the gold domes and striped towers that she'd only seen before in articles and picture books. And looming above them, more magnificent than anything else, was the Tapestry of Granity.

Its fabric was stretched over an enormous vertical platform, bigger than three tennis courts lined up together. Its long shadow covered the palace. And the figures woven into the cloth were so huge that even from this distance Legacy could make out the rectangular table and the senators sitting along it.

Legacy's heart began to miss beats. Just outside the city wall, she could see the white peaks of the tent where Van had told her the trials would be held. They looked as pristine and untouchable as the meringue on a fancy cake in picture books. That, Legacy thought, was where she'd have to win all her matches. She'd have to beat every kid from the provinces if she wanted to earn that academy spot.

Otherwise, she would have to return to her father in defeat. She would have to admit she'd been wrong. She'd have to watch Van go to work in a factory, and apologize to the littles for leaving them to pursue a fantasy about tennis.

Legacy tried to take a deep breath. For distraction, she looked back at the woven book and reread the chant for avoiding scorched eyebrows:

Running, leaping, flying, start, now you'll find your gentle heart.

It was a silly little rhyme, Legacy thought. But somehow it soothed her. She closed the book, repeated the words a few more times to stay calm, then gathered her pack and leaped off the cart.

Now the white tent rose before her. Beneath it, crowds of children and parents milled around frenetically. People from the city had come to watch, and they sat on raised benches encircling a long row of grass courts.

Swallowing her nerves, Legacy pushed past a group of parents to make her way to the registration desk. There, a harried woman with a snakelike braid coiled at the nape of her neck, gem-encrusted spectacles at the tip of her nose, and a giant blue ring on her finger explained that Legacy was to report to court fifty.

At court fifty, the woman explained, Legacy should wait in line until it was her turn to play the current occupant. Then, after four minutes, a horn would blow. If Legacy was ahead in the match, she'd move up to court forty-nine.

"You grind your way up," the woman said. "One court at a time."

Legacy listened while the woman went on, trying to make sure she didn't miss any important points. If she'd made it to the top court by two o'clock, the woman said, she'd play a final match. A final four minutes. The winner of that final match would be named provincial champion, and that's when she should make her pledge.

"Pledge?" Legacy said.

The woman glared. "Of loyalty," she said. "To whichever senator you'd like, though of course people usually make their pledges to Silla. But if you lose—on the top court or any other court on the way—you have to move down."

Legacy nodded, trying not to look frightened.

If Legacy lost on the bottom court, the woman explained, she was out. Then she should immediately return to whichever province she'd come from.

"No crying," the woman said, pursing her lips in disapproval, as if Legacy had already started displaying such unruly emotions. "And no complaining. We've had quite enough of that emotional provi behavior already."

Stung, Legacy moved away from the desk. On her way to court fifty, Legacy did pass a few kids sitting alone, tears streaking their faces. Some of them were wearing braided ponytails in imitation of Gia. Others were wearing paint they'd applied in imitation of other top academy players: elaborate lines covering their faces like Sondra Domenicu, or blue paint on their eyebrows like Villy Sal.

Legacy didn't have any paint. Nor was she wearing the imitation academy sneakers that some of the other kids had laced on. She only had her burlap shift and her warped wooden racket. Now she anxiously clutched it while she waited in line to step onto court fifty.

At the next sound of the horn, the loser—a flushed little boy with round cheeks and black lines on his cheekbones—ran off court in tears.

Legacy watched while his mother angrily followed behind him.

"This was the one chance that we had!" his mother was saying, grabbing his elbow. "And did I tell you to waste it?"

Ahead of her in the line for court fifty, a father was standing beside his young daughter, a skinny girl whose shoulders appeared to be trembling under her thin burlap shift.

"You play to his weakness," the father was saying. "You hear me? You bury him in the back of the court."

At the next sound of the horn, another little girl headed off court. Her face was already crumbling by the time her father knelt before her. Legacy winced in advance, but this father kissed the little girl's forehead.

His face was dirty with metium dust, and he wore a pair of refinery coveralls. "It's okay, Grazie," he said, tousling his daughter's loose curls. "You tried your best."

Legacy looked away. Standing by herself, without a parent to comfort or scold her, she felt lonely and grateful at once. There was no one to kiss her forehead, but there was also no one to make her feel nervous. She was as alone on the sideline as she'd been in the darkness of those early mornings, playing against the orphanage wall.

Or at least that's what she tried to remember when she finally stepped onto court fifty. If she focused on the feel of the grip in her hands, or the spot on the other side of the court where she wanted her shots to land, she could almost imagine that she wasn't playing a tournament match. Instead, once again, she was aiming for a divot in a stone on the wall, playing without fear, listening for the sound of the ball striking her strings.

Then the crowds under the tent disappeared, and she played as she always had: For the simple pleasure of playing. For the pleasure of counting her footsteps. For the love of the wind in her hair. For the joy of the *plonk* the ball made when it bounced on the soft earth.

By the early afternoon, Legacy had managed to make her way from court fifty all the way to the top five courts. She had a little trouble with a long-legged boy on the third court, whose limbs seemed to stretch from the baseline to the net, and on the second court she played a freckled girl, whose serve was so powerful that Legacy whiffed the first one completely. But she managed to beat them both nevertheless, and when the horn blew, signaling five minutes to two, she realized—to her amazement—that she had only one more player to beat.

She looked over the net. Her opponent had narrow eyes and wide shoulders. Her skin was dark as the burnt trees in the Forest of Cora, but her cropped hair was dyed silver. Waiting for Legacy's serve, she crouched low, narrowed her eyes even further, and shifted from one foot to the other.

Legacy paused. Suddenly the taste of metal filled her mouth, as if she'd bitten her cheek and drawn blood.

This was it: her one chance to go to the academy. The other courts had emptied out, and the remaining players had gathered around her court to watch. So had the tournament officials and the crowds of sight-seers who had apparently come out from the city. Their hair was braided in ornate patterns, and they wore lavish silks. They moved through the tent trailed by what must have been servants.

On a platform above the court, two announcers had taken their seats: it was Paula and Angelo, the same announcers Legacy had read about in the *Nova Times*. They announced all the major tournaments and were almost as famous as the players themselves. Paula was as elegant as Angelo was disheveled. She wore silks in bright colors

31

that complemented her burnished bronze skin, and her braids were gathered into a complicated three-cornered knot on top of her head. Angelo, on the other hand, looked perpetually rumpled. There was the shadow of a beard on his leathery face, and his graying hair was as mussed as if he'd only just rolled out of bed, grabbing his infamous flask on the way.

Above the announcers' platform perched a glass box where a group of people wearing even more elaborate silks—with extra drapes of fabric over their shoulders or jeweled belts on their tunics or narrow, shimmering pleats in their trousers—were sitting and watching. With a shock, Legacy realized they were senators. Then she saw the woman sitting at their center: High Consul Silla herself.

Legacy stared, gripping the tennis ball she'd been tossed. Silla! The woman who, single-handedly, had managed to get the old senators under control. She had once been the greatest tennis champion in the republic. They'd called her the Queen. And after her fame helped earn her a spot on the senate, she had put out the Great Fire by using her grana to summon a storm so powerful that it doused the whole forest for weeks, causing mudslides that slicked down into the prosite mines, but finally ending the fire that had devastated the country for months.

Sitting in the glass box, Silla looked younger than Legacy had imagined. She was wearing rust-red silk trousers and a matching silk tunic. Her jet-black hair was braided in hundreds of very thin braids, each decorated with gold beads, just as it always was in the pictures. Her skin was golden brown, but her eyes were dark and made even darker by the lines of black paint on her eyelids. They seemed to be staring straight back at Legacy, so that—for a moment—Legacy blushed.

Overhead, a voice blared through a loudspeaker. Paula was

announcing Legacy's name. "Here," Paula was saying, "we have Legacy Petrin, representing Foressa, the forestry province." For a moment, Paula paused to make a face, as though she'd smelled something disgusting. The crowd broke out into hoots of laughter, and Legacy felt her cheeks growing hot with embarrassment.

"She's playing," Paula continued, "against Jenni Bruno, representing Minori, the mining province." Then she made another face, and more laughter broke out from the crowds, and Legacy had to force herself to focus on her opponent.

Her shoulders were so wide, it seemed as if she'd have problems moving through doorways. Her face was bony and sharp, and her narrow, dark eyes sat close together.

With her silver hair, she looked less like a girl than a dragon. She also looked older than any of the other kids Legacy had played. Legacy wondered whether there was any way Jenni was young enough to have properly qualified for the tournament, until she noticed shimmery gray prosite dust under her nails.

So she worked in the mines, Legacy thought. And her hair wasn't dyed. It was silver because of the prosite.

No wonder her shoulders were so muscular. No wonder her face looked weary and lined.

She'd come out of the mines to play in the trials. And if she lost, she'd go back to the mines. She'd go back to those shacks and the slicks of silver mud dripping down into the darkness of those craters Legacy had passed on the way. She'd go back to the rare chance to ever come up to see sunlight.

For a moment, waiting for the horn to sound, Legacy pitied her. Then the horn blew. Legacy served, and Jenni launched her first return.

It was a blistering shot, faster and more brutal than any other return Legacy had faced in the trials. Legacy realized she was facing a formidable opponent.

Still, her pity for the girl had made her legs wooden. Her racket felt as heavy as metium ore. It was as if the air had gotten thicker. Taking a backswing was like hauling her racket through honey.

By the time she looked up at the scoreboard, she'd lost the first game. There were only two minutes left on the clock. And even so, Legacy wasn't sure she really cared. How, she wondered, could she justify stealing this girl's one and only chance to escape?

At least Legacy had a good place to go home to. She had a few more years, probably, before she had to go to work. Wouldn't the unselfish thing to do be to throw the match and let Jenni take the scholarship?

Distracted, Legacy glanced out at the crowd. The city dwellers were wearing silks woven with fine metal threads, shimmering gray and gold when they moved in the sunlight. Their jewels, and the complex braids they wore in their hair, made them look somehow hardened: as though they were statues come to life.

Why, Legacy thought, should she and Jenni Bruno—two kids from the provinces—be competing against one another to please all these living statues? Why should they beat each other into the ground to entertain these city dwellers, with their servants and the precious metal threads in their silks?

Legacy looked out at the crowd. They were pointing and clapping. They seemed perfectly delighted by the fine sunny day and the excellent match they were watching. But how, Legacy thought, could they be so cheerful? Did they not understand that if this girl with silver hair lost, she'd go back to a life underground?

And did they not understand that if Legacy lost, Van would lose the life that he'd dreamed of, and the littles wouldn't have enough milk in their bottles?

Legacy felt her former embarrassment turning to anger. The heat in her cheeks had migrated to her stomach and seemed to be spreading through her body from there. On the grip of her racket, Legacy's right hand began to feel hot. It was almost hard to hold on. She shifted her racket to her left hand. Then she blew on her right fingertips. She needed to get her anger under control.

But the better Legacy played, the more the crowd seemed to be enjoying themselves, and the hotter Legacy's anger burned. At the same time, her racket had grown a little lighter. The air had gotten thinner. Now, instead of hanging back on the baseline, she was moving forward, taking the ball at the top of its bounce, volleying whenever she could.

Somehow she won that next game, breaking Jenni's powerful serve. Even with her fingertips burning, she won the next one as well. And when the horn went off, Legacy looked up at the scoreboard and realized she'd won the match.

The crowd was roaring. The loudspeaker was blaring. Jenni was moving toward the net to shake Legacy's hand. And only then did she start to feel nervous. As Jenni approached her, Legacy could see the lines in her face, the tough skin on her hands, the silver nails cracked down to the quick.

What could she say, Legacy thought, to express to her that she was sorry? That she understood Jenni's plight? That she was only playing to save her best friend from the same fate, that she had an orphanage full of little children to care for?

By the time Legacy reached the net, her whole body was trembling.

35

And when she put her hand out, Jenni clutched it so hard that Legacy felt the bones in her fingers crowding together.

"I'm sorry," Legacy stammered. "I—"

Jenni leaned close to Legacy's face. "Sorry?" Jenni said. "*Sorry?* The only thing you should be sorry about is if you don't win the nationals."

Legacy looked up at her in surprise.

Jenni glared back. "If I'm going back to the mines because of you," she said, "you better win. And when you lift up that trophy, you do it for me. You do it for the rest of us provis."

Then Jenni was moving away, and flashbulbs were popping. Someone grabbed Legacy's arm and asked her to whom she pledged her loyalty. The crowds were roaring so loudly she had trouble hearing her own thoughts, but she took one knee as she'd seen players in the papers doing, looked up at Silla, and thanked her for the opportunity she'd provided.

Then Paula and Angelo posed her with a trophy. Flashes went off on all sides. Paula prodded Legacy's ribs with her elbow and murmured that she should turn her head. "Show the better side of your face," Paula said. "And smooth out your hair."

Surprised, Legacy tried to pass her hand over her hair. It was loose, as it always was: when she ran, Legacy liked to feel the wind running through it. Now she realized how unkempt it must seem to all the city dwellers with their ornate braids. Suddenly embarrassed again, she felt heat beginning to creep into her face, but Angelo had already grabbed her other arm, and then they were leading her away from the tent, moving toward the towering walls of the city.

CHAPTER FOUR

THE TAPESTRY OF GRANITY

A t the city gates, Legacy and the crowd of announcers and photographers passed easily through the checkpoints. Once they were inside the city, Paula had to nudge Legacy several times to keep up as they headed along the small winding streets toward the palace, and Legacy felt the urge to stop and look around in amazement.

She had to stay alert not to get in the way of the horses and the carts rounding corners on two wheels, rushing past her with the sound of clip-clopping hooves on cobblestone, or the bicycles that whizzed by, ringing their bells, or the street sweepers with their brooms, clearing orange peels and paper napkins out of the gutters.

Everywhere Legacy looked, crowds of people were milling around. The men wore their hair close-cropped or shaved, as they did in the provinces, but here all the women wore braids. More complicated styles, it seemed, were a mark of distinction. A woman in turquoise silks with an upside-down braid that started at the nape of her neck and culminated in a fan on top of her head rushed out of a jewelry shop and nearly knocked Legacy down. A girl with a single small braid on one side of her lank hair was selling red roses. On the stoop of a fishmonger shop, a bald baby was crying. On both sides of the streets, enormous striped-stone towers spiraled up into the sky.

Gazing up at their forbidding facades, Legacy thought that the stories she'd heard of the Senate Wars must have been true. Back then, when the old, corrupt senators were fighting one another with grana, devastating one another's provincial estates with forest fires, floods, dust storms, and blizzards, there were also vendettas in the streets of the city. Apparently front doors were too risky. So were regular houses. Everyone in the city who could afford to, built colossal stone towers without any doors, and instead of entering the usual way, they used ladders to climb into windows.

Now, gazing up at the towers, Legacy imagined senators standing at the little arched windows, gazing out on the provinces to make sure their estates hadn't been damaged.

Of course, the Senate Wars had been back in the old days before the Great Fire, before Silla put it out and reformed the corruptions of the senate. Now the streets were safer. And business—in the city, at least—had clearly picked up again.

Legacy and her entourage crossed a bridge marked with a stone sign that read "Butchers' Bridge." The bridge was lined on both sides with butcher shops, every window full of skinned animals hanging from big iron hooks. After the bridge, they continued on to the central part of the city, where every block was crammed with bustling storefronts. Hawkers called from the doorways. The illuminated windows displayed glass lampshades, wooden horse figurines, paper threaded with metals, gumdrops, scimitars, gold bracelets, and lemon-shaped soaps.

Legacy was so focused on avoiding the bicycles whizzing by and the hawkers luring her in that she didn't even see the palace rising on the crest of the hill.

Then, suddenly standing in the courtyard before it, she dropped her head back to look up. It was the most enormous building she had ever seen.

The palace rose higher and higher above her, built of giant blocks of yellowish stone. The longer she looked up at it, the taller the palace seemed to grow. And the taller it grew, the smaller Legacy felt, until it almost seemed as if she'd shrunk to the size of an insect.

She was already dizzy when she turned to the other side of the courtyard and realized she was looking up at the Tapestry of Granity. Her mouth gaped, and she heard a gasp of astonishment escape her open lips.

She'd seen pictures, of course. And Van had told her all about how it worked. But now, standing below it, she realized it was so much more magnificent than she'd dared to imagine.

There, towering above her on a tapestry the size of several tennis courts lined up together, were the senators. Their silks were depicted in shimmering threads: lapis blue, carnelian red, amethyst green, and dusty rose. They sat along a wooden table, their hands folded before them, their silks undulating ever so slightly: the effects of the breeze, maybe. Or maybe the threads faintly changing.

This was it, Legacy thought. The great gift left to the Republic of Nova by its original founders: a tapestry woven from metal threads that resonated with the minds of its people, depicting the leaders in whom they had faith.

Every two years, as Legacy and Van had read in the history books they found in the attic, any citizen of the republic who could make it into the city assembled in that very courtyard—the place Legacy was now standing—to look up at the tapestry.

39

Once the ceremony began, people simply had to imagine a leader who inspired confidence. Then, as Van had explained to her several times, the minerals in the threads absorbed and reflected the will of the people. The picture began to shimmer and shift until the figures of the hoped-for senators had materialized in the fabric. Once they'd been depicted in the tapestry, those senators then began a new term of power.

Now, in the sunlight of the midafternoon, the colors of the tapestry were especially brilliant. Legacy could make out glints from the mineral threads woven into the colored silks. These, as Van had explained, were reflectors: Threads woven with strands of metium, prosite, revidian, corasite. Threads that absorbed and reflected the emotions of the people who beheld them. They shimmered and gleamed so that the figures almost seemed to be made out of water. They were flowing, moving, alive. If Legacy stepped to the left, she felt as if the senators' eyes were following her. And if she headed back to the right, they followed her that way as well. When a breeze rippled the material, the skin on the senators' arms seemed to shiver.

In their silks, with their symbolic totems, their ornate braids, and their glimmering jewelry, all the senators cut striking figures. But none of them was more impressive than Silla. She sat at the center of the long table, occupying the high consul position, which she'd held since she put out the Great Fire. Now, all these years later, she filled it in regal fashion. In her usual style, she wore a long, rust-red silk robe over her matching tunic. Her braids were beaded with gold. One of her eyebrows remained slightly arched, as though daring anyone to believe that anyone other than her could keep the republic united.

Even the announcers seemed cowed in the presence of her image. "There she is," Paula whispered, nervously touching the three-cornered knot on top of her head. "The woman responsible for your scholarship."

"I'm very grateful," Legacy said.

Paula narrowed her eyes at Legacy and pursed her painted lips, as though that hadn't been a properly humble response. Confused, Legacy tried to stammer a few more appropriate words, but Paula had already turned and was making an announcement to the photographers. Then the flashbulbs were flashing again, and Angelo prodded Legacy toward the front door to the palace, which swung open and shut, leaving Legacy alone in the entrance.

Suddenly she was surrounded by silence. Above her, the cavernous entrance hall stretched nine stories high, curving toward a painted dome overhead. All around her stood doors, balconies, stairs, and more doors.

But which one was she meant to enter? Where was she supposed to go to start training?

She was still standing there, trying to decide what to do, when she heard the *clip clip clip* of footsteps crossing the marble floor. Then, around a massive stone pillar, she caught sight of a girl who looked to be the same age as Legacy, though she was much shorter. Her coppery red curls had been parted at the center and styled into two braids that were fastened at the top of her head, her enormous eyes were bright green, and her little nose was scattered with freckles. She was wearing a snug black jacket and wide-legged black pants.

The girl grinned. "Leg!" she said. "I'm so excited you're here!"

Leg? Legacy thought.

But the girl was already hugging her. Legacy stood awkwardly in her embrace. "You don't mind if I call you Leg, do you?" the girl was saying.

"I've always just gone by Legacy," Legacy said, though even as she said it she realized it sounded strange to her own ears. She'd heard it so many times today, over loudspeakers and in the mouths

41

of strangers, that she almost wondered who that name referred to.

"My name's Pippa," the girl said, enthusiastically pumping Legacy's hand. "Actually, it's Pippiana. Pippiana Spago."

Then she set off at a fast clip, so that Legacy had to hurry to keep pace behind her. "You might recognize my name," Pippa said, glancing over her shoulder and giving Legacy what she must have meant to be a significant look, "because my father's famous. He's Silla's stringer."

Stringer? Legacy thought. She'd never even heard the word. It hadn't shown up in the books she'd read about Silla's years as a player.

In a doorway to the rear of the grand entrance hall, Pippa stopped and turned. "But don't be intimidated," she said. "I'm not a snob. And you don't have to call me Pippiana. My friends call me Pippa."

"Sure," Legacy said.

"I mean, I have a lot of friends already," Pippa said, furrowing her brow and gnawing on the cuticle of her thumbnail. "But still, maybe you could be my friend also?"

"Sure," Legacy said again.

"I knew it!" Pippa said. Then she delivered another one of her crushing hugs, which Legacy endured until Pippa led her through the door, still enthusiastically chattering. "I knew we'd be friends," she was saying. "As soon as Silla came back from the trials and announced that you'd won them, I thought, 'I think we'll be friends.' Then I thought, 'Maybe we'll even match!' And that's why I volunteered to show you the palace."

Legacy was focusing so hard on trying to keep up with Pippa's chatter that it took her a moment after moving through the open door before she registered the view that had spread itself in front of her. There, stretching into the distance, were the most beautiful tennis courts Legacy had ever seen.

There were rows and rows of them, terraced up a long hillside. Their grass was perfectly clipped. The white lines were newly painted, and the nets hung shining and taut on the net posts.

"Ta-da!" Pippa said, grinning up at Legacy.

Legacy couldn't move. She couldn't talk. She had a thousand questions to ask, but Pippa was charging ahead.

"That's the main court," Pippa said, gesturing at the court closest to the palace. "That's where you'll play the nationals. And that's the stable." She was pointing to a long stone building to the side of the courts. "You'll need a good pyrus to train with, of course, because that's how you'll develop your power, and—"

"Hold on," Legacy said, finally finding her words. "Did you just say *pyrus*?"

"Of course," Pippa said, furrowing her brow.

"But, I thought—"

"You thought they'd been banned," Pippa said. "Fire hazard and everything."

Legacy nodded. She hadn't just thought they'd been banned—she thought they'd been extinct for years. She only knew of them from the Cora stories she read to the littles, or expressions people sometimes used in the provinces. Steamy summer days, for instance, were "hot as a pyrus sneeze." But Legacy had never imagined that there might still be living pyruses.

"Look, Leg," Pippa was saying. "There's one thing you need to get straight. Some things that are banned in the provinces are allowed here at the academy. I mean, you can't get as good as Gia training against *backboards*."

"So that stable's full of *pyruses*?"

"It sure is," Pippa said.

"But can you ride them?" Legacy said. "Like in the Cora stories?"

"Are you kidding?" Pippa said. "They're too temperamental for that. They'd buck you off in a second. Then they'd incinerate you into a pile of ash. We just use them for training. Mostly they breathe fireballs, and you have to learn to return them."

"So, what, if I'm going to compete against the best players, I'm supposed to just go into the stable and pick out a pyrus?"

"No, no," Pippa said, setting off again, this time toward a garden to the side of the palace. "The builders handle the pyruses. It's part of their job. They might not be the brightest bulbs in the box, but even they can't just lift weights all day."

"Builders?" Legacy said. "What's a builder?"

Pippa stared. "You've never trained with a builder?"

Legacy shook her head.

"Oh boy," Pippa said, whistling softly under her breath. "Well, they'll help you get physically fit. It's essential to get the right builder. That's something you can control, even if you can't choose which stringer you match with. Your builder will work out with you when you're not training with Polroy. He's the head coach, just like my father's the head stringer. Argenti's the head grana instructor."

Legacy nodded, trying to take it all in.

"But the builders also get the pyruses out of the stable," Pippa said. "It's a whole system they know with whistles and signals. That's the main reason why you've got to get a good builder. They'll help you get a good pyrus."

"Got it," Legacy said. She had about a thousand more questions, but Pippa was still trucking ahead, and Legacy was struggling to keep up.

"Also, Leg," Pippa said, glancing over her shoulder. "Do me a favor. Don't tell anyone you've been reading Cora stories, okay? You'll have

44

enough trouble around here without people thinking you're some kind of religious fanatic."

"Trouble?" Legacy said, but Pippa cut her off.

"That," she said, "is the hedge maze." She was pointing toward an enormous wall of green leaves. "And beyond that's the Garden of Fears. Don't go in there at night. And make sure you never get lost in the hedge maze."

"Why shouldn't I go in there at night?" Legacy said.

Pippa, who was busy pointing out other landmarks, ignored her. "That's the cafeteria," she said, gesturing toward a closed door. Then she climbed a staircase built of marble so old the stone had been worn underfoot, so that it seemed to have softened, like warmed butter or honey. "And that floor," Pippa was saying, "has the gym. That floor has all the classrooms: you know, memory, concentration, and grana. And the next floor's for the stringers. The top floor is strictly forbidden; that's where my father's workshop is. And the seventh floor is the bedrooms."

Legacy's head was spinning by the time Pippa led her down a hall and showed her to her bedroom. Still, she was rattling on about her father's stringing workshop and the importance of matching with a good stringer. As Pippa's words washed over her head, Legacy felt her nerves beginning to froth in her stomach. She told herself to calm down. The injunction didn't help. Pippa's words were now blurring together, and Legacy racked her brain for something that might help her calm down and listen more clearly. Then she remembered the chant for avoiding scorched eyebrows. She closed her eyes.

Running, leaping, flying, start, she said to herself. *Now you'll find your gentle heart.*

She opened her eyes. Even though Pippa was still rattling on, she felt calmer. She'd have time, she told herself, to learn about matching with a good stringer. She'd have time to figure out what happened in a grana class. In the meantime, she needed a pyrus. And to get one, apparently, she needed a builder.

First things first, she said to herself, *you've got to get a good builder.*

Pippa smiled. "Well, that just about does it," she said. "You're probably tired, so I'll leave you alone."

"Thanks for the tour," Legacy said, extending her hand, but Pippa dove in for another one of those bone-crushing hugs.

"See you tomorrow, Leg!" Pippa said, then started off down the hallway.

"It's Legacy," Legacy called after her, but Pippa was gone.

———

Legacy pushed open the door to her room and then paused. It felt as if she'd snuck into someone else's bedroom. Everything was so different from the room where she'd slept with the littles. The bed, for instance, was the size of a boat. And instead of a threadbare blanket, it was covered in a rich red brocade.

There were no maps of secret cities on the ceiling. Instead, the stone was draped with tapestries. One depicted kids playing tennis. Another showed Silla as a young girl. Legacy recognized her at once. She was playing tennis on the academy courts, using her grana to summon dark clouds. On the opposite side of the court, rain fell like swaths of dark gauze over Silla's opponent.

Suddenly Legacy was overcome with exhaustion. She realized she hadn't had a moment to sit since she'd hopped out of the chicken cart early that morning. She hadn't had a bite to eat since she'd played her first match on court fifty.

Now her legs felt like jelly. Taking a seat at the edge of the bed, she gazed at the tapestry and the rain falling on Silla's opponent.

That was the kind of grana the top players in the country could summon. They all knew how to transform what the announcers at exhibition matches were always calling their "inner weather" into real weather patterns. Gia, for example, could summon darkness. Villy could summon snow. Sondra Domenicu could cause little earthquakes. Now, sitting on her new bed, Legacy realized that all the kids at the academy probably had some kind of grana. But Legacy had never caused any change in the weather.

Of course, Legacy thought, the other kids' grana wouldn't be as strong as Silla's. Since the Great Fire, Silla's new regulations had limited the strength of players' grana. She didn't want them to be used by feuding senators to start another natural disaster.

According to Van, who reported what he read in the *Nova Times*, all the academy players now used standard strings in their racket. Some how, that kept their inner weather from reflecting outward too fiercely. Even the best players, like Gia, could only slightly alter the atmosphere in the courts. Once, Legacy saw her play in an exhibition match in Agricio, and the darkness she summoned wasn't consuming. You could still see the ball. You could still see the net. And Sondra shook the earth only slightly. Villy caused only light flurries of snow to eddy down on his opponents.

But even so: Legacy didn't have any grana at all. Remembering that, her nerves started frothing again. This whole adventure, she thought, was completely misguided. What was she doing here, in this strange, luxurious room? Who did she think she was, coming all this way to compete against the country's best players? How could she

47

possibly win the nationals if she didn't even have any grana?

Legacy couldn't sit still any longer. She stood and stretched for a moment. Then she unpacked her flour sack and placed her warped racket under her bed. She put *The Book of Muse* in her bedside table. And when she opened her closet, to her surprise, she found row upon row of shining rust-red academy dresses. The fabrics glittered with shimmery mineral threads, all of them cut in the most fashionable styles: sleek long sleeves and pleated skirts. On the floor there were pyramids of golden tennis balls and a row of rust-red academy sneakers.

Legacy ran her fingertips along the various fabrics. She'd never worn anything but her burlap shift. All the provis wore burlap; only city dwellers could afford to wear silks. She couldn't even imagine herself in one of these new outfits. She'd look like a new person, she thought to herself. She'd almost *be* a new person.

Then she peered into the back of the closet and saw the Tempest.

There it was: the racket she hadn't asked for.

She stepped closer. There was a note tied to its neck:

For the newest member of our academy family. Thank you for joining us. Warmly, Silla

Legacy tried to take a deep breath, but she felt something pressing down on her shoulders. She'd felt it before, when her father had given her sneakers she knew he couldn't afford: the weight of obligation, heavy as a big coat.

48

How could she ever pay Silla back for all this generosity? She didn't even want to guess how much that racket cost, with its shining black frame and its woven strings coated in brand-new red wax. When she picked it up, its weight made her feel jumpy and nervous. To calm down, she put it back in the closet and returned to her bed.

Closing her eyes, she repeated the spell for avoiding scorched eyebrows. Then, when she opened her eyes, she noticed a stone cat poised on her mantel. It was so lifelike that Legacy couldn't help but approach it to touch its pointed ears. She was reaching forward when suddenly it leaped off the mantel, hissed at Legacy, and escaped under the crack in Legacy's door.

Legacy's mouth fell open. Had she really just seen that? She was sure that cat had been made of stone. And the crack under the door was no wider than an inch!

Settle down, she said to herself. *Now is not the time to start seeing imaginary cats slipping through cracks.*

But her heart was still beating alarmingly quickly. It took repeating the chant several more times while eating her last corn cake for Legacy to relax enough to feel tired.

Finally, she pulled back her luxurious covers. The big, boatlike bed was as soft as a cloud, and it had been a long day. Just before she fell asleep, she remembered those terraced courts and the stable beyond them.

First things first, she reminded herself. *You have to get a good builder.* Soon after that, she was asleep, dreaming about hedge mazes and stone cats, butchers' bridges and iron hooks, tapestries and winged horses.

49

CHAPTER FIVE

A SPIDER-SHAPED
SCAR

It was still dark when Legacy woke. She blinked for a few moments, getting used to the darkness.

Then she realized that something was wrong. The ceiling wasn't white, and the map of her secret city was missing.

Instead, she saw drapes of rich fabric and walls covered with brilliant tapestries. Then she remembered where she was.

Her heart ached for her father, who would have discovered her disobedience yesterday morning. She longed for the littles. She wished she could walk past Van's bed and see him sleeping with one of his enormous books on his chest. She wished she could slip outside and play tennis alone, on the back wall of the orphanage garden.

But then she remembered those rows of courts, stretching up the terraced hillside. And she remembered her goal. *First things first*, she said to herself. *Get a good builder so you can train with a pyrus.*

For a few moments, Legacy stood in her closet, examining her rows of new tennis dresses. They were all so fancy, with frills and ribbons and pleats. She felt strange putting them on just to play tennis, as though she were putting on a ball gown for breakfast. Or wearing a bathing suit to

50

walk in the forest. Instead, she pulled her burlap shift over her head and reached for the Tempest.

But that, too, made her feel strange. It was so light and clean, and just touching it sent a jolt of energy up Legacy's elbow.

Startled, she put it back down. She told herself she'd switch rackets when she'd gotten a little more comfortable at the academy. For now, she pulled the old warped wooden frame out from under her bed. As soon as she lifted it, and fit her hand to the black handprint on the grip, she felt more like herself.

After lacing up the battered old sneakers she'd brought from home, Legacy grabbed a tennis ball and headed down the marble steps and out the back door. Outside, it was still so dark the sky hadn't yet been tinted blue, but late enough that the stars had gone out, so it was hard for Legacy to see where she was going.

Even so, as she walked along the endless rows of grass courts, she could make out the shapes of a few players already practicing. But as she studied their moving forms, she realized they weren't practicing with each other. They weren't hitting against walls. They were playing against horses.

The animals flew back and forth along the baseline, flapping their enormous wings, breathing flaming tennis balls.

"Pyruses," Legacy whispered. But these weren't the pyruses she'd read about in the Cora stories. Or maybe they were the pyruses she'd read about, when they were getting attacked by hungry lurals.

While they moved back and forth on the baseline, their eyes shone red. Their ears bared back. Their dilated nostrils puffed thick smoke that made Legacy think of the factories she'd passed yesterday.

Nervously, Legacy skirted the courts. When one of the kids took a break to drink water, she edged closer.

"Um, excuse me?" she said. Her tone sounded pathetic, even to herself.

The kid turned and glared. "What are you looking at, provi?" he said.

"Looking?" said a girl wearing a Gia braid, barely pausing on her way back to the palace. "More like lurking."

Legacy's face was stinging with embarrassment as she hurried off toward the more distant courts. She noticed that some of the kids were wearing rust-red academy clothes, and others were wearing black warm-up suits that swished as they walked on the sidelines.

Maybe those, she thought, were the builders. Then she tried to approach several of them as they passed, but each time, they shook their heads and hurried off in the direction of the stable. It took three or four tries before she finally caught one.

"Excuse me," she said, tugging the tissue-thin sleeve of his suit.

The kid turned. Legacy noticed that his head was shaved, and there was a spidery pink mark on the deep brown skin of his neck.

Legacy drew her hand back. It was hard not to stare at that mark. It almost looked as if he'd been burned, or maybe branded.

"What do you want?" the kid said.

"I just—" Legacy stammered, forcing herself to look away from his neck. "Are you a builder, by any chance?"

"I am," the kid said. His arms were crossed over his chest.

"Do you want to be *my* builder?" Legacy said, wincing at how pathetic it sounded.

The kid snorted. "Already taken," he said. He headed off again toward the stable.

Legacy clenched her fists. How was she supposed to get a builder?

They all seemed determined to ignore her. And if she couldn't get a builder, how could she get a pyrus, and how could she train harder than everyone else so she could beat them at the championships?

Glancing down the long row of courts, Legacy saw a few kids playing on a backboard. She remembered the scorn in Pippa's voice when she'd said, *You can't get as good as Gia training against* backboards.

But what else could she do? There weren't any old stone walls near the courts. The only fence she could see, standing between the courts and the hedge maze, was a long iron gate with thin spindles. All she wanted was to practice. And wasn't that what she was here for?

In frustration, she dropped the ball she'd brought out from her room and slammed a forehand drive toward that iron gate.

It hit a thin spindle and bounced back.

Legacy caught it. Then she smiled.

She knew how to do this. She'd done it every morning, when she chose a particular divot in a particular stone. Now she focused on that narrow iron spindle. With her next shot, she hit it again. Then she did it again.

For a while, she rallied that way. She imagined the narrow spindle was Gia, counted her footsteps between shots, and focused hard on that metal point, until she became aware that someone was watching her. She caught the ball and turned.

It was the kid in the black tracksuit, with the scar on his neck.

"Pretty good accuracy for a provi," he said.

Legacy looked at the mark. It was, she realized, the exact shape of a spider: the brand that was given to thieves and their families before they were banished.

The realization startled Legacy enough that she couldn't help continuing to stare. The kid touched his neck. He laughed a hard, unhappy laugh that almost sounded more like a cough.

"Never seen one of these?" he said.

Legacy reddened and looked down at her feet.

"Not even in all your years in the sticks?" he said. His voice was cutting.

"I'm sorry," Legacy said. "I didn't mean to stare."

"But you did," he said. Then he headed back toward the courts. His shoulder brushed hers when he passed.

By the time the bell rang, signaling the beginning of morning practice, the sun had risen. It cast a cold light over the palace and the grass courts.

Legacy joined the other kids on the bleachers. Players in rust-red academy clothes were stretching their shoulders, sitting alongside builders in their black warm-up suits. To one side of the bleachers, a group of kids with braids just like Pippa's—two of them, fastened on top of their head—had recently arrived. Like Pippa, they were wearing little black jackets and wide-legged pants. Pippa was among them, jumping up and down, frantically waving to get Legacy's attention.

Legacy smiled and waved. Those, she assumed, must be the stringers. They'd lined up on the sidelines to watch, and Legacy noted that, over their jackets, they were wearing necklaces with large stones set over their chests. Many of the stones shone like cat's-eyes—rust red; topaz; cornflower blue—but a few of them were dark and opaque.

Among the players who had gathered on the bleachers, all the girls had braided their hair, whether it was long or short, curly or straight, black or red or blond or brown. Some wore their own styles, but a large group of them wore their hair gathered into a single long braided ponytail, in the style of Gia. These girls even wore two lines of black paint on their cheeks, as Gia did when she competed.

It was this group of girls who was especially cold when Legacy tried to sit with them. And even when she left their group and found a place far away, she could still feel their eyes on her back. When she heard them laughing, she had a feeling they were laughing at her.

Maybe it was her wooden racket, Legacy thought. Or her unbraided hair or her burlap shift. But everyone—not just the Gia crew—was cold to her when she tried to be nice. More than once, she overheard kids calling her "provi." Maybe it was because they all came from the city, but they seemed to be united against her.

For that reason alone, Legacy was excited when a man sauntered out in a rust-red warm-up suit and announced that they'd spend the morning running sprints. This, Legacy assumed, must be Polroy. Pippa had said he would be the head coach. He was a big man, with burly round shoulders and a wide smile.

"Listen up, kiddos," Polroy was saying, pacing in front of the bleachers. He had a loose-jointed walk, so that he seemed to amble like a big bear. Occasionally, he smiled up at the players. "The qualifying tournament is in three weeks. You've got twenty-one days to get ready for your one chance to prove that you're up to playing against the elites. So this morning I want you to run like your life's on the line. I want you to run like this is the last shot you'll be given."

Despite Polroy's somewhat ominous word choice, Legacy smiled to herself. She might have never trained with a pyrus, but she'd been running sprints on the hill up to the orphanage as long as she could remember. When Legacy joined the other kids lining up on the baseline, getting ready to sprint, she was nervous, but she was also excited. If there was one thing she knew how to do, it was run, and run fast.

So it was surprising when the whistle blew and she felt the other kids pulling ahead of her. She saw them gaining ground. By the end of the morning, she hadn't won a single sprint.

When Polroy blew the whistle for lunch, the other kids headed off to the cafeteria. Legacy lagged behind, feeling defeated.

"Don't worry, kiddo," Polroy said, passing her on his way in. "You're still soft. But you'll toughen up quick. It'll be easier once you've gotten a lural."

A lural? Legacy thought. She remembered the Cora stories, and the illustrations of those ferocious animals with spotted hides and sickle-shaped fangs. *They have those, too?*

"But . . . but how do I get one?" Legacy managed to sputter.

"Same way you get a pyrus," Polroy called over his shoulder. "Gotta get a builder."

Then he sauntered off, his warm-up suit swishing. Legacy watched while he slung an enormous bear arm around another kid's shoulder.

"But how do I get a builder?" Legacy said, mostly to herself because Polroy and the kid he was talking to were already gone, the cafeteria door having slammed shut behind them.

CHAPTER SIX

PERFECT MEMORIES

In line at the cafeteria, waiting for lunch, Legacy could feel the Gia crew's eyes burning the back of her head. It felt as though they were watching her every move, waiting for her to make a mistake.

And it wasn't only the little Gias. Everyone seemed to be avoiding her or laughing behind her back. No one talked to her on her way in, and no one helped her figure out how to get her tray, or why there didn't seem to be any plates or utensils, or how to navigate the line to pick up her food.

Legacy felt her lip trembling, but she reminded herself that she hadn't come here to make friends. She'd come to win the nationals and keep the orphanage open. To do that, she had to train harder than anyone else. And if she was going to do that, she'd need to get some food in her stomach.

She set to work filling her tray. Moving along the buffet, she examined all kinds of food that she'd never seen before. There definitely weren't any corn cakes or hunks of wild honey. Instead, everything came in the shape of packets, smoothies, and bars. Legacy eyed packets of recovery goo, chocolate-cherry endurance bars, bottles of orange tennisade, and bright green muscle-bulk smoothies.

It all looked disgusting—like food one of the littles had chewed up and spit out. Legacy had to force herself to grab a few options, her stomach turning slightly with each additional packet she placed on her tray.

As soon as she moved away from the line, she was confronted with a swarming rust-red sea of players. They sat on one side of the cafeteria, and a black sea of stringers filled the other. A bunch of builders in their black tracksuits occupied a few tables at the far end of the room.

Standing in the middle, holding her tray, Legacy felt her face getting hot. Where was she meant to sit? Which table was she supposed to join?

It was clear that she was meant to sit with the players, but somehow she'd managed to be one of the last players to leave the cafeteria line, and most of the seats were already taken.

It seemed to Legacy that everyone else had obeyed an obscure seating pattern that they understood and she didn't. In the orphanage, everyone had sat at one big table together. Here, everything was divided according to some inexplicable system. It was as though everyone else in the cafeteria had received an instruction manual from their city-dwelling parents, a code of behavior that she'd never learn to decipher.

One table, for instance, was entirely full of little Gias: tall Gias, short Gias, dark Gias, and light Gias. And there, at the head, perched Gia herself. It was hard for Legacy not to stare at her. She'd seen so many pictures of Gia: in Van's *Nova Times* or in the set of greasy old tennis cards she and Van had found for sale at the market. But this was the first time she'd seen her in person. On Legacy's tour of the palace, Pippa had explained that the elite kids trained alone, on secret courts set off from the others. But, clearly, elites and qualifiers ate at the same tables.

Now Gia sat straight-spined at the head of the table, with her long honey-blond braid, her tawny skin, and her stripes of black paint. She stared directly at Legacy, and her almond-shaped eyes narrowed so that Legacy made no mistake about the fact that she was not welcome to sit at that table.

Looking at Gia, Legacy's hand crept up to her own hair. It still wasn't braided. She'd gotten distracted by everything else, and she hadn't even remembered to pull it back into a ponytail. Her burlap shift was drab and saggy compared to Gia's sleek academy dress. And her unpainted face was so plain.

Legacy forced her eyes away. Behind Gia's table sat a group of boys who looked like Villy Sal. And there he was, as well: the kid ranked number two in the country. His tennis card said that he was the child of silk merchants and that he could summon snow. In person, he looked older than he did on his card: a muscly teenaged boy with a gleaming black pompadour, pale skin, and eyes that were startlingly blue. He, too, stared at her as though he already knew he despised her.

Beyond Villy was Sondra Domenicu's table. Sondra, the oldest girl at the academy, was ranked number three in the country. She was famous for her accuracy. That, and the fact that she could make the ground shake and rumble when she played, so much so that sometimes little cracks appeared in the court. Legacy recognized her trademark style from her tennis card: she'd pulled her thick black hair into two braids that fell over her shoulders, and she represented her grana with a jagged black line of paint that cracked her deep brown face down the center.

Some of the other players at her table wore similar lines, and all of them looked a little bored with the lunchtime routine, like they'd been at the academy for some time. Many of them were wearing recovery sleeves on their elbows or ankles, and some of them were icing their shoulders or wearing heat packs strapped to their necks.

And then there was a table of what seemed to be the general misfits: three kids alone at a big table, glancing anxiously around the cafeteria. There was a rabbity boy with round glasses, a girl so thin she seemed as if she might disappear, and a scared-looking boy who kept sucking on his inhaler. But even those kids shifted uncomfortably in their seats as Legacy approached. And when she reached them, the thin girl threw her red academy jacket over the remaining empty seats.

Legacy stopped. Then she swallowed her pride. "Could I sit with you?" she said. She'd started to hate the sound of her own voice.

The girl's eyes darted toward Gia's table. Then she shook her head.

"Can't risk it, sorry," she whispered, then focused very hard on an empty bottle of orange tennisade.

Legacy had begun wondering whether she was allowed to take her food outside, where she could be alone, when she spotted the builder with the spider-shaped brand on his neck. He was sitting alone at a table at the back of the cafeteria.

When Legacy joined him, he didn't look up. He was sipping a muscle-bulk smoothie, and he seemed to be very absorbed in an article he was reading in something called *Muscle Magazine*.

"Listen," Legacy said, unwrapping an endurance bar. "I'm sorry for staring earlier. It's not like I really fit in around here either."

"Who says I don't fit in?" the boy said without looking up from his article.

Legacy felt her cheeks burn even hotter. She kept getting off on worse and worse starts.

"Sorry," she said. "Let's start over. I'm Legacy Petrin. Nice to meet you."

"Javi," the boy said. He flipped the page.

"Listen, Javi," Legacy said. "What do I—"

60

"Can't do it," Javi said, interrupting her. "Full docket. I'm already building too many qualies."

"Qualies?" Legacy said.

"Qualifiers," Javi said. "I don't take more than two."

Legacy glanced around the cafeteria. Most of the players were qualies. Only the top six were considered elites, and a quick head count revealed far fewer builders than qualies.

"But if you can't take on more than two qualies," Legacy said, "how do all the qualies have builders?"

"Who says I can't take on more than two qualies?" Javi said. "I just don't want to. I'm the second-ranked builder at the academy. My qualies perform well, so my stipend's one of the highest. Why would I risk my income on some newbie from the provinces?"

"Because I'll work harder than anyone else," Legacy said. "And because I plan to win the nationals."

Javi snorted. "So does everyone else in this cafeteria," he said.

Legacy gritted her teeth. "If you won't be my builder," she said, "I'm going to get a pyrus myself."

"Idiotic," Javi said.

"Why?"

"They're vicious. You try to get one yourself, you'll get incinerated on the spot."

Legacy opened a packet of green-grape recovery goo. The food was actually delicious, despite what it looked like. While she ate, she examined the stringers on the other side of the cafeteria. They were eating in relative silence, at least compared to the more boisterous players. Many of them read books at their tables. Some of them quietly fiddled with little webs of red string that they'd pulled taut between their fingers.

And all of them wore those heavy-looking stones around their necks.

Legacy was about to ask Javi about the stones when she was distracted by Pippa. She was moving away from the lunch line, holding her tray, heading toward the tables of stringers.

She looked significantly less sure of herself than she had when she was taking Legacy on the tour of the palace, letting Legacy know that her father was famous. Now she was glancing around, apparently unsure of where to sit. Her stone was a dull black, much less impressive than the other stringers' glowing red ones. And every time she tried to sit down, the other stringers shook their heads or covered the empty seats with their hands.

Legacy felt a pang of sympathy. "Why don't they like her?" she said.

"Talks too much," Javi said, without looking up from his magazine. "Like someone else I know."

"About tennis?" Legacy said.

"About everything. Tennis, strings, Ancient Stringing Craft. You name it, she'll talk about it, like she's the world's expert. And while she's at it, she'll tell you about her famous father. About how he's Silla's favorite. About his forbidden workshop. About how lovely their villa is on the hill and how happy her family is in their perfect villa. The only thing she *won't* talk about is how she's been at the academy since she was five and she still hasn't matched with a player."

"What's wrong with stories about a happy family?" Legacy said.

Javi made a face. "No one here wants to listen to stories about happy families," he said. "No one cares about all her happy memories."

"Is it such a bad thing that she has happy memories?" Legacy said.

"We're not here to be happy," Javi said. "Pippa should know that."

Legacy thought for a moment. Then she gave herself another squirt of recovery goo. "All I know," she said, once she'd swallowed, "is that if I grew up with my family in some fancy villa, I'd talk about it too. If I had perfect memories, I'd want to think about them whenever I could."

Javi snorted. "No one here has perfect memories." Then he pointed to the rabbity boy with the glasses. "That one there? His mother used to shake him till his glasses broke if he lost a match she thought he should win."

He pointed to one of the Gias. "And that there? Her father tells the press she's a brat."

Finally he gestured toward Villy Sal. "*His* father was throwing fire-balls at his head when he wasn't much more than a toddler. You might think it sounds mean, but that's how these kids get so good. You don't get drive from perfect memories. You get drive because you have something to prove, and you won't give up till you've proved it."

Legacy was still considering this when Pippa caught her eye. She started maniacally waving, beaming so hard Legacy worried her face might crack open.

"Ignore her," Javi muttered, staring hard at his *Muscle Magazine*. But Pippa was already approaching.

"Leg!" Pippa said, sitting down at the table. "How'd the first day go?"

Legacy put down her recovery goo. "Okay, ground rules," she said. "It's Legacy, not Leg."

Pippa ignored her. "D'you really get a free Tempest?" she said. "Rumor has it Silla gave you a Tempest, because after seeing you at the trials, she thinks you'll beat Gia."

Legacy stared. "How—"

"Polroy told us," Pippa said. "After the trials. You should've seen Gia's face when she heard! She looked like she'd swallowed a mouse."

So *that* was why Gia hated her, Legacy thought.

"Let's see it," Pippa said. "You have it with you?"

Legacy shook her head. She kept her wood racket under the table so she wouldn't have to explain how she'd chosen to use it instead.

"She doesn't have it," Javi muttered, still looking at his *Muscle Magazine*. "She's using some junky wood racket, and she's holding it under the table."

"Let me see," Pippa said.

Legacy pretended she hadn't heard. She focused, instead, on opening up a packet of s'mores recovery goo, but she could feel Pippa watching her.

"My opinion," Pippa said, "is that you should ditch the wood racket and use the Tempest. Even with the standard stringbind, there are enough reflectors in the strings and the frame for you to express grana. And there aren't any reflectors in wood."

"No kidding," Legacy said. She could feel Pippa still watching her.

"What is it, anyway?" Pippa said.

"What's what?" Legacy said, squirting an experimental blob of s'mores goo onto her finger. It was brown and goopy and definitely did not look delicious.

"Your grana," Pippa said. "What is it?"

Panicked, Legacy took a deep breath and filled her mouth so full of s'mores goo that she couldn't answer, hoping to at least buy herself some time while she swallowed.

"She glows," Javi said, in a bored tone of voice, flipping the page of his magazine.

Legacy stared at him.

"She glows?" Pippa said.

"Sure," Javi said. "Little aura of light around her head when she's focusing hard. I saw it this morning, when she was hitting against the hedge-maze fence."

Legacy realized she'd swallowed the goo without even tasting it. Javi saw an aura of light around her head when she was playing against that iron spindle? Was that what Van had seen also, when he'd watched her practicing against the orphanage wall? When she thought the sun was rising, but he said that it was still night?

She wanted to ask Javi more about what exactly he'd seen, but Pippa was whistling softly.

"A light grana!" she said. "That's very rare. Why didn't you summon it when you were at trials?"

Both Javi and Pippa looked at her expectantly. Legacy took another squirt of s'mores goo and decided it was actually amazingly tasty.

Javi sighed and looked down at his magazine. "She doesn't know how to summon it," he said. "Figures, what with the education you get in the provinces."

"Oh, well," Pippa said, faking a smile, "you'll learn. Of course, we haven't seen any light grana since the Standard Stringbind was effected. Though, of course back in the days of Ancient Stringing Craft—"

"Please," Javi said, "don't start in on Ancient Stringing Craft."

"Ancient Stringing Craft," Pippa said, glaring at Javi, "is an important aspect of our history, even if it *has* been banned. Even now, it's essential for us to know how it worked. Otherwise, why would Silla fund my father's workshop—"

"Oh, we all know about your father's precious workshop," Javi said, flipping a page.

Pippa flushed. "I was *talking* to Leg," she said.

"It's Legacy," Legacy said.

"And anyway," Pippa said, "we *don't* know about my father's workshop. That's the whole point. Only *he's* allowed access to Ancient Stringing Craft materials. That way there's no danger of students meddling in the old ways."

"Sure," Javi said.

Pippa glared at Javi. Then she turned to Legacy. "That's the way Silla wanted it to be," she said. "Honor the history of Ancient Stringing Craft, but make sure it stays in safe hands."

"You've met Silla?" Legacy said. Even after seeing her face in that glass box, it was still hard for Legacy to believe that Silla actually existed in real life and wasn't just a mythical figure on the Tapestry of Granity.

"Of course!" Pippa said.

"Has everyone here met Silla?"

"Oh, not . . . everyone," Pippa said.

"Just special people, like *her*," Javi said, rolling his eyes.

Pippa ignored him. "She's very busy," she said. "And of course after the assassination threats, she mostly keeps to herself. But she's magnificently generous. She gave you your spot, didn't she? She's always supporting everyone. Gia's stringer has a sick mother, you know, and Silla's single-handedly undertaking the expenses of her medical treatments. And Gia herself, you know, was an orphan. Silla took her in. She's lived at the academy since she was an infant. Even the cats," Pippa said, gesturing toward the two orange cats sunning themselves on the windowsill. "Silla adopted them, too. As if it wasn't enough to stop the Great Fire and end the Senate Wars and reform all the old abuses!"

Javi flipped a page. He didn't seem particularly moved by Pippa's list of Silla's generosities. Legacy glanced again at his scar. She wondered whether that might have something to do with how he felt.

"You don't agree?" Legacy said.

Javi ignored her.

"He doesn't care if it's not lining his pockets," Pippa said, making a face. "All the builders are like that."

"Not all of us grew up in a villa," Javi said.

"Not all of us care about who has a villa," Pippa said.

"Some of us don't have the luxury of not caring," Javi said.

"Some of us don't think 'not caring' is a luxury!" Pippa said.

"Some of us are *businessmen*," Javi said.

"Some of us are *artists*!" Pippa retorted.

"Please," Javi snorted, flipping another page. "Don't talk to me about art. Now that Ancient Stringing Craft's out of the picture, all stringers do is tighten or loosen the strings, depending on whether rain's in the forecast. Stringers aren't artists. They're weathermen with fancy necklaces."

"At least we're not musclehead materialists," Pippa said.

Javi laughed his hard cough of a laugh. "Speaking of materials," he said, "why don't you tell her why your stone still isn't glowing?"

Pippa's nostrils flared. Then she turned to Legacy. "You know why the builders won't take you?" she said. "Because they only train players who bribe them. Parents send gifts, or extra money to add to the stipends, and the builders take on extra kids."

Legacy felt her face go cold. "So that," she murmured, "is how you get a builder."

Pippa went silent. She looked down at her tray. "I'm sorry, Leg," she said. "I didn't mean—"

Legacy was considering the grain in the wood of the table. On her lap, her hands had clenched into fists.

"Don't worry, Leg," Pippa said, "we'll figure something out. I'll ask my mother for extra allowance, and we'll find a—"

Legacy stood up.

"I told you already," she said. "It's Legacy. And I don't need any help. I'm getting a pyrus myself."

Then she tucked her racket under one arm, ignored the glares of the Gias, returned her tray, pushed open the cafeteria door, and set out for the stable.

CHAPTER SEVEN

SCORCHED
EYEBROWS

To get into the stable, she heaved open a massive wood door, sliding it sideways along rollers. Then she entered the shadowy darkness within.

The gloom was so thick that it took several seconds for Legacy's eyes to adjust. Before they did, she could smell hay. The scent reminded her of the barn at the orphanage, where they'd kept their goats. Realizing that, Legacy smiled. She'd always loved the goats, with their big trusting eyes, their hard little skulls, and their knobby legs.

But when Legacy took a step into the darkness, she realized that these were no goats.

To her right, through the iron grates in the stall doors, the cold blue eyes of the lurals glinted brightly in the blackness. As she passed, the creatures bared their teeth, showing their gleaming white fangs.

To the left, in individual stalls, were the pyruses: an endless row of horses with wings. There must have been hundreds of them, Legacy thought: their bodies a little smaller than regular horses, their giant pink wings bristling behind them. They were pawing the stone floor of the stable and snorting plumes of dark smoke, each looking angrier than the next.

They glared out through the grates of their stalls, their eyes red and unblinking.

Suddenly, Legacy thought, the idea of bribing a builder didn't seem quite so out of the question.

Some of the pyruses flapped their heavy wings, as if preparing to rush at Legacy's head, but their fetlocks were shackled by heavy iron chains that jerked them back whenever they tried. In frustration and rage, they bared their big yellow teeth.

Legacy took a deep breath and willed herself to keep moving. She kept a safe distance from the doors of the stalls, remembering the fireballs she'd seen before morning practice. Only when she came to a stall in which the pyrus seemed to be sleeping did she stop and slowly approach.

Curled up on the stone floor, with its legs pulled underneath its body, this pyrus looked less intimidating than the others.

Its gray coat was in bad shape. The fur had been worn thin by the shackles it wore, so that pale pink skin showed underneath. But a white blaze ran up its nose, and a white patch of fur spread over its chest. Up close, Legacy could see that its wings were faintly fuzzy.

It almost looks cute, Legacy thought, ducking to her left to avoid a fireball breathed by a pyrus in the next stall.

This is the one, she said to herself, looking down at her curled, sleeping pyrus.

Then she took a deep breath, stepped forward, and began to open the door.

In an instant, the sleeping pyrus's eyes flew open. Its nostrils flared. Its ears flattened. Before Legacy had time to slam the door shut, it had flown toward her with a shriek and sent a fireball straight at her face.

Legacy just managed to duck, but she felt a searing pain across her left temple.

The pyrus's chains snapped it back so violently that its body slammed against the back wall of the stable. Then it pulled itself up again and seemed to be preparing to emit another fireball when Legacy heaved the door shut.

Shaken, Legacy lifted her hand to her temple. She winced. The skin had been burned. She was lucky the blast had missed her eye.

And her eyebrows. Something chimed in Legacy's mind. The chant for scorched eyebrows! It had seemed so odd when she read it in *The Book of Muse*. Back then, on her way into the city, sitting with those scared chickens, she'd had no reason to imagine that very soon she'd be facing a fire-breathing winged horse. Now Legacy wondered whether that chant was the trick.

It was a long shot. She knew that. But she didn't have any better ideas. In a slightly trembly voice, she leaned toward the grate in the door and started to chant:

"*Running, leaping, flying, start,*" she said, "*now you'll find your gentle heart.*"

The pyrus's expression didn't look any less angry. But it cocked its head to one side, and its ears pricked up a little. Its hoof stopped scraping the floor. It was obviously listening.

Legacy swallowed. She licked her dry lips and tried again:

"*Running, leaping, flying, start; now you'll find your gentle heart.*"

Now the pyrus's eyes had gone a little less red. It blinked at her twice and tapped the stone more gently with its foreleg.

71

Legacy took a deep breath. She reminded herself that she was here to win the nationals and save Van from going to work. She pushed open the door of its stall.

"*Running, leaping, flying, start,*" she said. "*Now you'll find your gentle heart.*"

She kept saying it, again and again, while she edged toward the pyrus. When she leaned down to unlock its iron shackles, she felt its hot breath on her neck. It smelled rotten and smoky, like charred hay and carrion, and Legacy tried not to breathe in too deeply or to let her mind wander to what might happen if the pyrus turned on her in this instant, while she worked to unlatch the iron chain.

Once she'd managed that, she reached for the pyrus's bridle. It shied away from her at first, but she repeated the chant again, and it allowed itself to be led.

Her heart beat hard in her chest while Legacy walked with her pyrus toward the door of the stable and led the creature into the sunshine. She was nervous, but everything was going fine until, midchant, she tripped on a root and fell forward, yanking the pyrus's bridle.

She felt the whole weight of the animal shying away from her. Then the bridle slipped from her grasp, and when she turned toward the pyrus again, what she saw was so terrifying that she forgot the words to the chant.

There was the pyrus, unfurling its wings with a terrible whoosh. Its eyes glowed as red and furious as they'd been in the stable.

Then Legacy was running for her life, sprinting away from the barn and over the courts, with the sound of wingbeats whooshing behind her. The first fireball grazed her left arm. She felt a stab of pain near her elbow. The next only just missed her right shoulder, and she was still

72

sprinting, aware of the smell of burning burlap, when she realized she couldn't outrun it.

There was no use running away. She had to do something to face it.

She had no time to come up with a plan, so she simply stopped in her tracks. She turned and crouched, tucked her forehead low to the ground, and covered the top of her head with her forearm.

"*Stop!*" she shouted. "*Sit, Pyrus!*"

She squeezed her eyes shut. Then she crouched even lower, shielding her head with her arm, hoping at least to protect her face from the flame she was sure was coming.

But nothing happened. The sound of the pyrus's beating wings had gone silent. All she could hear was some strange piping sound, like a wooden flute.

Confused, Legacy opened one eye, then the other, and looked around.

Javi was holding a whistle, standing next to the pyrus. And the pyrus was sitting on its haunches, its wings folded, looking at Legacy with an obedient, gentle expression.

For his part, Javi was surveying Legacy with something like admiration.

"You," he said, "are an idiot."

Legacy swallowed. Her left arm throbbed. Blisters were forming on the red welt.

"You're also the fastest sprinter I've ever seen," Javi said.

"Did I get that pyrus to sit?" she said. "Or did you?"

"You did," Javi said.

"And the whistle?"

"To keep him calm."

Legacy shook her head. So she'd stopped the pyrus? Just by telling him to sit? "How did I—?"

"I don't know," Javi said. "But I think I might have room for you on my docket."

Even the pain in Legacy's arm couldn't keep her from grinning. "You'll be my builder?" she said.

"Can you train now?" he said. "Or do you need a bandage?"

"I'll train," Legacy said.

"Good," Javi said. He walked on court, and the pyrus rose and followed him.

"Volleys," he said.

Legacy moved up to net. As Javi called out instructions, and the pyrus launched fireball after fireball straight at her face, she did her best to volley them, defending her face with her racket.

The fireballs moved faster than any shots she'd returned off the orphanage wall. Before she'd returned the last one, another fiery shape was leaving the pyrus's mouth.

But Legacy did her best to keep up. And as she returned more and more volleys, her confidence grew. She thought again of how Javi had said she was the fastest sprinter he'd ever seen. She thought of that morning, when she'd hit ball after ball against a single iron spindle.

The more confident Legacy felt, the more easily she returned the volleys. The more easily she incorporated the advice Javi called out. It was as though her racket were getting lighter. As though the air around her were thinner. A few times, her returns were so powerful that the pyrus had to duck away, lifting his wing to avoid getting smashed on the snout.

They trained like that for more than an hour, until Javi looked at his watch and called her to stop. On the sideline of the court, he bandaged her burn with a fresh roll of gauze and handed her a packet of strawberry-pie recovery goo.

Javi watched her while she ate.

"Pretty good volleys," he said. "Pretty darn good for a provi."

Legacy looked up at him. She felt a spark of warmth in her stomach: it was the first time someone at the academy had complimented her. And for that matter, it was the first time anyone who didn't have a reason to—her father, say, or her best friend—had given her a compliment. She felt the spark of warmth spread through her body as a soft glow. She had to keep herself from goofily smiling.

"Pretty good advice for a musclehead," Legacy said.

Javi grinned. "We'll get you fit in no time," he said. "Now we just have to match you with the right stringer."

Legacy gazed off toward the palace. A door opened on the sixth floor, and a row of stringers—wearing their fastened braids, dressed in their little jackets—exited and walked single file along a narrow balcony. They looked so small, high up and close to the ramparts, like a row of little black crickets. Legacy still didn't understand what they did, or what it meant to match with a stringer.

"Sure," she said, hoping her uncertainty didn't show in her voice. "Just gotta match with the right stringer."

CHAPTER EIGHT

THE
VELVET-LINED BOX

O n their way back to the stable, Javi glanced at Legacy.

"You still don't know, do you?" he said.

Legacy tried to look casual. "What?" she said, reaching out to pat the pyrus's muscled shoulder. He glared at her with red-rimmed eyes, and she flinched away.

"What it means to match with a stringer," Javi said.

Unable to help herself, Legacy let out a sigh of relief. "I thought no one would ever explain!" she said. "People around here seem to just expect me to know everything they know already!"

Javi rolled his eyes. "Like they'd know how to live in the provinces," he said.

Legacy shot him a grateful smile, and while they rolled back the stable door once again and led the pyrus back to his stall, Javi began to explain how the stringers watched the players on court. He explained how a stringer's stone started glowing when she watched the player she was meant to match with.

It had something to do—Javi said—with the cords of the stringers' necklaces and the minerals in the stone. They only resonated with the inner weather of the right player.

"*What is* this 'inner weather'?" Legacy said. "People keep talking about it."

Javi shrugged. "It's basically just another word for emotions," he said, leading the pyrus into his stall. "We call it 'inner weather' because it's the source of the external weather events that players cause. So Gia's inner weather, for instance, corresponds to the darkness she summons. The whole process is grana: the ability to manifest inner weather."

"And there are minerals in the strings," Legacy said, "that allow players to express?"

"Not in *those* strings," Javi said, nodding toward Legacy's warped wooden racket. "But they're in the strings of the Tempest. All the Tempests are woven with the standard stringbind. It's pretty basic: just a small sample of all the reflectors involved with expression. The stringbinds used to be individualized to allow players to express maximum grana. But now no one can express like they used to. The stringers have to talk a big game so they don't feel useless. But at the end of the day, grana doesn't matter anymore. It all just comes down to training."

Legacy nodded, and Javi handed her a currycomb. While she brushed the pyrus, taking care to stay far away from his angry, smoking face, Javi cleaned out his hooves and finished the subject of matches. When a match was made between a stringer and a player, he said, the resonance caused the stone on the stringer's chest to start glowing. That signified a connection between stringer and player that would last as long as the player stayed at the academy. From that point on, the stringer was responsible for tending the strings in their player's racket.

"So the stringers weave the standard stringbind?" Legacy said, running her hands through the pyrus's mane.

Javi shook his head. "Nah. The rackets come with the standard stringbind. Now the stringers just tinker. They loosen and tighten the strings, depending on the weather. They're not even allowed to re-coat the wax."

Legacy was starting to get exasperated. She almost wanted to paw the stone floor with her own hoof in frustration. "But if the stringers just tinker," she said, "why is it so important to match with a good stringer?"

Javi shrugged. "It makes no sense to me, either. But all the top players have stringers that everyone says are brilliant. You can't get to the top without a good stringer. Plus, they're going to be with you for every practice and every match. And when you have a big match coming up, you'll want a stringer who keeps you calm. Not, in other words, someone like Pippa. Not someone who's always yammering on about nothing."

Javi finished shackling the pyrus. Then he and Legacy stepped back, letting themselves out the door of the stall. The pyrus watched them go. His eyes were still lined with red, and he didn't look particularly friendly, but Legacy was so grateful that he had refrained from burning her face off that she thought she should try to give him another pat.

"Don't," Javi said. "They're hungry. They bite."

Legacy pulled her hand back and looked at the pyrus from a safe distance. She hated to see how his heavy collar had worn his fur bare at his neck. She remembered how she'd felt at the orphanage, when food was short for the week and she went days with her stomach grumbling.

"Does he have a name?" Legacy said.

"They're not pets," Javi said. "And anyway, you're not here to make friends with a pyrus. You're not here to make friends, period. You're here to win the nationals."

"Sure," Legacy said. But still, she didn't move toward the sliding door of the stable. This was the first normal, friendly conversation she'd had here. She didn't want it to end.

Javi glanced at her sideways. He seemed to understand. But still, he heaved open the door and stood back to let her go through it.

"Remember that," he said. "You're not here to make friends. Go back to the palace. Get some dinner. And get a good night of sleep. You have a long day of training tomorrow."

The next morning, when Legacy awoke, she knew where she was. She didn't expect to find the map of her secret city, or the long row of littles sleeping beside her.

This time, remembering how all the kids had stared at her in the cafeteria, and how self-conscious she'd felt about her burlap shift, Legacy put on one of the academy outfits: a rust-red skirt with a matching tank top. She pulled her hair into a ponytail. For a moment, she thought about braiding it, but no one had ever taught her to braid: in the provinces, girls wore their hair loose. She sighed. The ponytail, she told herself, would have to do for now.

Then she looked at her wooden racket, propped alongside the Tempest, and remembered what Pippa had said at lunch: *There aren't any reflectors in wood.* Instead of picking up her wooden racket, she reached for the Tempest. Even if—as Javi said—grana didn't matter anymore, she couldn't afford to risk it. If there was a chance the Tempest would help her express her "inner weather," she had to take it. She needed all the help she could get.

The Tempest was lighter than her old racket. The grip almost seemed to vibrate in her hands, and for a moment, feeling the tremors as far up as her elbow, Legacy wondered whether it wouldn't be better just to stick with the old racket. At least she knew how it played.

But then Legacy remembered the littles, and her father praying, and how she'd disobeyed him and abandoned him to come to the academy. She set her jaw. Now wasn't the time to be sentimental about an old wooden racket.

Then, taking a deep breath, Legacy stuffed her old racket in the trash can. She felt a pang of guilt, looking at the handle sticking out of the trash. There was her familiar handprint on the grip, which Van had fashioned out of soaked bark. She'd loved that racket for so many years, playing with it every morning on the back wall of the orphanage.

Still, she forced herself to turn away. When she went out to the courts, she was carrying the Tempest.

For a few hours, in the dark, she and Javi trained with the pyrus. The fireballs he breathed were like comets searing an orange arc through the darkness. Then there was a line of matching orange on the horizon, and by the time the sun had risen, the stringers had filed out of the palace and lined up by the courts. They were still waiting there when Polroy sauntered out to start morning practice.

"Okay, kiddos," he said. "This morning we're playing matches. Newest kids on the bottom court. Top kids on the top. Winners move up. Losers move down. Try not to stay at the bottom."

Legacy swallowed her nerves and marched to the bottom court, taking in the stringers along the way. They seemed to have been instructed to stand in a regal, dignified fashion. Only Pippa was moving. She seemed to be trying to simultaneously stand still and frantically wave at Legacy, a combination that made her look like a wriggly puppy.

Somewhat embarrassed for Pippa, Legacy glanced at the stringing instructor. She'd heard a few kids call him Lucco, in hushed tones of respect. Now he stood at the end of the line, wearing a tailored black suit and a silvery scarf. He was tall and strikingly elegant, with green eyes and white-streaked hair that was combed so that it waved back from his temples. Legacy couldn't believe it: That man was Pippa's father? They didn't seem related at all. While Pippa wriggled and waved, her father shot her such a look of irritation that Legacy's heart went out to Pippa.

But she remembered Javi's advice: *You're not here to make friends.*

Then she headed to the bottom court and focused on her first opponent.

He seemed to be several years younger than her, but it looked to Legacy as if he'd been at the academy a long time. Long enough, at least, to have started styling his hair in a Villy Sal pompadour. Long enough that he'd had plenty of time to train with a pyrus.

Or at least that's how it seemed, because he was attacking every shot as though it were a fireball heading straight for his precious hairdo. He threw his whole weight into every ball, roaring with each shot he hit, pumping his fist when he won a point.

Legacy was startled by his aggression. It got her off-balance. She felt like a butterfly pinned to the baseline, permanently on the defensive. Even though the Tempest was lighter than her old wooden racket, it still felt too heavy, and when she struck the ball, the force of her opponent's shot ricocheted up her wrist and vibrated into her shoulder.

"Move forward, kiddo," Polroy called from the sideline. "Get on the attack!"

Legacy flushed. She didn't want Polroy to see her play badly. So far, Polroy had been the only adult at the academy to take any interest in

81

her. Even though she'd failed so miserably at sprints on the first day, he'd still taken the time to give her advice. This was her chance to redeem herself, now that he was standing at her court, ignoring everyone else.

So were a group of three or four stringers, including Pippa, all of them with dark amulets. They were watching her play, Legacy realized, to determine if she was their match.

Her opponent won another game. Each time he won, he pumped his fist and roared. Legacy felt as though she were sliding downhill, trying desperately and failing to claw her way back to the level. At last, Polroy blew the whistle. Legacy's opponent moved up, casting a victorious glance over his shoulder, and Legacy stayed on the bottom court.

That's how it remained all morning, until Legacy heard a commotion in the cluster of stringers. Pippa yelped, and when Legacy turned, she saw that Pippa's amulet was glowing faint red.

Legacy's stomach dropped. Pippa looked overjoyed. She was trying and failing not to jump up and down, waving a thumbs-up in Legacy's direction.

Polroy chuckled. He patted Legacy's back with his bear paw. "Looks like we've got a matching ceremony to perform," he said.

Legacy left her racket on the bleachers and followed Polroy to join the group of stringers. Lucco joined them as well. He cleared his throat and began to read from a battered leather book. There were a few lines about resonance in the strings and the expression of inner weather, and then Lucco took Legacy's hand and placed it on Pippa's.

Legacy couldn't help noticing how unhappy he looked. He almost seemed ready to throw down his old book and storm back to his workshop.

If Pippa noticed, however, she didn't show it.

"I knew it, Leg!" Pippa whispered during a lull in her father's incantation. "I knew you were my match! Didn't I say so? Right from the start?"

Legacy tried to force a smile, but she remembered again how Javi had said that a good stringer should calm down her player. And there was Pippa, grinning and wriggling around like a puppy.

Legacy's smile must have wavered, because suddenly Pippa looked hurt.

"We'll be great together, you'll see," she whispered, but her voice didn't sound quite so certain.

"Sure," Legacy said. She hoped she sounded excited, or at least more excited than she actually felt, which was as though she'd swallowed a hunk of metium.

Even as she walked away from the ceremony, she still felt heavy and cold. She'd almost reached the cafeteria when another stringer—a tall girl with hunched shoulders and little, birdlike eyes—caught up to her and handed her the Tempest.

"Don't leave your racket around, provi," she said. "You never know who might take it."

Legacy started to thank her, but she'd slipped into the cafeteria.

Later, when Legacy had filled her tray and found Javi at the back of the cafeteria, she asked him about the tall girl.

"She's Gia's stringer," Javi said. He didn't look up from his muscle magazine. "A real pro. Best stringer at the academy."

Legacy took a sip of her muscle-bulk smoothie.

"Speaking of stringers," Javi said, turning a page, "I hear you matched with Pippa."

Legacy nodded.

"You idiot," Javi said. "Didn't I tell you to match a good stringer?"

That night, in her room, after stumbling through afternoon classes, another training session with Javi and the pyrus, and another harrowing meal in the divided cafeteria, Legacy was too tired even to change out of her shiny new outfit.

She threw herself down on her bed fully dressed, closed her eyes, and tried not to feel like a failure.

But she'd done so badly in that morning's practice. And then she'd matched with the one stringer no one else wanted.

Legacy opened her eyes. Even the cat that was now sitting on her windowsill and archly licking its paws seemed to disapprove of her performance.

So far, Legacy thought, her only success at the academy had been getting the pyrus. And she'd only been able to do that because of a chant she learned from *The Book of Muse*.

Since arriving at the academy, she'd been too busy to take it out of its drawer. Now she pulled it out. When she opened it, the note from Van fluttered out. Legacy read it again: *Think of me when you're famous!* Legacy could imagine him cracking up as he wrote that. She could imagine him in the attic, reading that book on mining mechanics, with *The Book of Muse* on his lap. Now, when Legacy lifted it closer to her face, her smile widened. Its cover smelled like Van: stale corn cakes, grubby fingers, and ancient rolled-up tapestries. But her smile faded when she turned through a few pages.

Something had happened. The pages were harder to read. Some of the stitches must have unraveled. A few of the pages were empty.

Legacy stared. Only days earlier, riding the cart into the city, she'd been able to read all of the pages. Some of them had been faded, of course, but now she couldn't even make out the spell to avoid getting scorched eyebrows. The only page that was still perfectly clear was the diagram of a proper pyrus mount.

Looking at the diagram again, Legacy felt a creeping sensation, as if there were spiders crawling over her neck. Because—in careful stitches—the diagram depicted the precise manner in which she'd crouched before the pyrus when she told it to sit.

It showed the embroidered figure of a girl touching her forehead to the ground, holding one arm over her head. There were various other markings, as well: measured angles, rays pointing from the girl to the pyrus, strange incomprehensible symbols. Legacy couldn't understand all the marks, but it was clear that the page was depicting the very pose she'd taken, the pose that had caused the pyrus to calm.

Either by accident or because somewhere in the back of her mind she'd retained a memory of the diagram, she'd followed its instructions. And that had allowed her to calm the pyrus when it was getting ready to scorch her.

Legacy stared at the book. Maybe, she thought, it was full of all the other instructions she needed to train at the academy, the secrets she needed to win the nationals.

But now she couldn't read it. Desperately, she flipped through a few more blank pages. She felt tears rising to her eyes. How had this happened? How could the pages have faded in only two days in her drawer?

For comfort, Legacy tried to hold on to her Tempest, but it wasn't the same as her old racket. Its grip didn't have the shape of her hand. Its weight wasn't the old, familiar weight.

Legacy got up from her bed and went to the trash can, where she'd

85

stuffed her old racket this morning, but even before she looked inside she felt her stomach sink. The racket wasn't there. The trash can had been emptied. Someone must have cleaned her room while she was out.

Now the tears spilled over Legacy's cheeks. And the fact that she was crying only made her feel worse. Up until now, she'd managed to keep it together. Even in the cafeteria, when no one let her sit at their table. Even when she'd learned that people got builders with bribes. Even when she'd lost at sprints and got crushed in the matches.

But now that she'd finally let herself cry, Legacy felt her unhappiness brimming up to the surface of herself. How was she supposed to succeed in this awful, unfriendly place? How could she win the championships and earn the money she needed to justify having abandoned the littles? How could she justify losing her old racket and disobeying her father, who loved her?

Legacy was crying hard—her shoulders shuddering, her breath coming in uneven jags—when she heard a knock at her door. Then, finally, she forced herself to stop. The knocks were getting louder when she shoved the book back into its drawer. Whoever was out there was really battering the door when Legacy straightened out her rumpled outfit and finally answered.

She found Pippa, grinning. Pippa held up a small, square wooden box with a complicated gold clasp. "I thought maybe we could get to work on your racket!" she said.

Legacy tried to swallow her irritation. "Listen, Pippa," she said. "Do we have to do it tonight? I'm really tired."

But Pippa had already stepped past Legacy into the bedroom. Seeing her, the cat on the windowsill stopped licking its paw and leaped into the darkness.

"This morning," Pippa was saying, "when you were playing, it seemed like something wasn't quite right with your racket. Like it was hurting you or something." She plonked herself down on Legacy's bed and opened her wooden box. The inside was lined with red velvet and fitted with about fifty tiny silver tools. They looked like various types of miniature can openers and corkscrews.

"I'm guessing you were feeling some vibrations in your elbow," Pippa said.

"A few," Legacy said, watching Pippa cautiously.

"I can work on that," Pippa said. She picked up the Tempest and turned it over, focusing on the strings. "Of course, in the old days, when we used Ancient Stringing Craft, I could have done more."

She plucked the Tempest's strings with her finger, one by one, then bent her ear to the strings, as if listening for faint music.

"In the old days, you know, stringers got to know their matches so well they wove individualized stringbinds. The old stringers could weave their players' stories and secrets into the strings."

She glanced up at Legacy. "Of course," she said, "not everyone knows this. Books on Ancient Stringing Craft are all banned. I just happened to find a few old books my father had lying around."

Legacy had to restrain herself from rolling her eyes.

"I shouldn't even be telling you this," Pippa said, "but now that we're friends, I think we should share secrets, don't you?"

Now she was looking up at Legacy so hopefully that Legacy forced herself to smile politely. In response, Pippa grinned enthusiastically, then picked up her stream of chatter again.

"In the old days," she said, "stringers used to be artists of players' inner weather. They represented it so well, using different mineral threads, that the players' emotions came out in every single shot they hit. Stringers didn't even have to watch matches to know that they'd strung the racket right. They could *hear* it. They watched matches with their eyes closed. They listened to the sounds the ball made when it hit the strings, and if the music was harmonious, they knew they'd woven the strings right. If the music was out of tune, they knew they'd made a mistake."

Listening to Pippa, Legacy closed her eyes. She knew it was absurd, but she almost felt as though she could hear music coming from the Tempest as Pippa plucked its strings.

"That's why players' grana was so intense," Pippa said. "When they played, they could summon blizzards and tsunamis. Mudslides and fires. Then it was a problem, because senators were using the players who had pledged their loyalty to increase production on their estates. They'd cause it to rain more, or less, so that the olive trees produced better olives. And they'd cause fires, or droughts, to eliminate other senators' crops. That's what caused the Great Fire. And that's why Silla banned the use of nonstandard stringbinds. Also amplifying botanical waxes. Now everyone plays with the same stringbind. Everyone uses the same non-amplifying red wax."

Soothed by the regular rhythm of Pippa's chattering, Legacy began to nod off, until the tilt of her own head jolted her awake. Then she stifled a yawn. She was so tired. What she needed, she thought, was to get some sleep before training tomorrow. Not to hear a lecture on Ancient Stringing Craft.

But Pippa was still caught up in the history of stringing at the academy. "Now," she said, setting Legacy's racket down and reaching into her wooden box to remove a little silver clamp and a pair of silver pliers no bigger than a nail clipper, "we're limited by the new rules. And of course we're not really supposed to know all the details about Ancient Stringing Craft. But I think it's important, even so—"

"Listen, Pippa," Legacy said, stifling another yawn. She was starting to get the feeling that Pippa would talk all night if she let her. "Maybe we could—"

"I just like to know how it worked," Pippa went on, ignoring the interruption. "I don't see how it hurts. I also don't see how it could hurt for us to get to know one another. Maybe we could even be friends."

Legacy sighed. Pippa was looking up at her with a heartbreakingly hopeful expression. It reminded her of the expression that she had so often seen on Van's face when he was presenting her with a new scheme about winning the national championships.

And that—she reminded herself—was why she was here. Not to make friends with overprivileged city dwellers.

"Listen," Legacy said. "Pippa. No offense, but like I said, I'm really tired."

Pippa's face fell. She looked back down at the Tempest.

"Okay," she said. "No problem."

"Maybe another time we can share secrets," Legacy said.

Pippa produced a small smile. She stood, brushed off her black jacket, and plucked Legacy's strings one more time.

Her brow furrowed. "It's just—they really don't sound right . . ."

"Tomorrow," Legacy said, trying to make her voice both firm and gentle. "Tomorrow we'll make sure they're wound right."

"Sure," Pippa said. "It's just—if you're going to play against the elites, you'll have to learn how to express grana, and I'm not sure—"

"*Pippa!*" Legacy said, no longer able to conceal her irritation.

"Right," Pippa said. "Sleep. I get it."

89

Then she hurried off, and Legacy was left feeling guilty and ashamed of herself. But she was so tired. She knew that she couldn't stay awake all night feeling guilty if she needed to play well in the morning.

Later, while she was still lying awake, trying and failing to sleep, she wished she could follow the lines of her secret city map, as she had when she was agitated back home. Instead, in the darkness, she kept thinking about what Pippa had said about strings and inner weather and grana.

Pippa was right: if Legacy was going to have any chance of beating players like Gia, she'd have to learn to express grana. And the truth was, she had no idea how to do that.

CHAPTER NINE

FLIGHT

Even if summoning grana was still a mystery to Legacy, her tennis was definitely improving.

After a week of training every day with Javi and the pyrus, Legacy had begun to feel stronger. She was getting used to aggression. Twice a day, she spent hours returning fireball after fireball. She learned to take shots earlier. She learned to throw her weight into each stroke.

At night, after dinner, Javi had her out on the courts again, working on a new training technique he'd been developing in secret. They worked under cover of darkness, since it was a departure from official academy protocol. "Academy training protocol has to do with repetition and drive," he said. "Specifically drive based on fear: fear of failure, fear of losing your spot. Fireballs flying at your face. Lurals running behind you. That's all fine. It's extremely effective. It's the easiest way to build drive. But I've been thinking: What if you also trained in a way that tapped into pleasure? Freedom and exhilaration?"

Then he pulled a contraption out of his backpack that looked like a horse harness attached to a giant silk tent. Once he strapped Legacy in, he had her running sprints with the kite wind-borne above her, billowing in the darkness like an enormous moth. It pulled her along—her feet barely touched the ground. She ran so freely and so fast it felt as if she were taking flight.

"It's like flying!" she called out to Javi.

Javi rolled his eyes. "Let's not get carried away," he said. "You're just getting the feeling of speed in your muscles." Then he ordered her to run more sprints, timing her with his stopwatch and jotting notes in his training notebook.

The next night he gave her sneakers he'd built with wheels in the soles. And the day after that, he set up a huge trampoline on the court, so that with each step she took forward to volley, she leaped forward, attacking it so early it caused her to laugh out loud in exhilaration.

By the beginning of Legacy's second week at the academy, when Polroy had the qualifying kids—the "qualies," as they were called—play morning matches, Legacy wasn't startled anymore by her opponents' power. She could handle it. With a week left to go before the qualifying tournament, she regularly found herself climbing up toward the top courts.

And there was another development, as well, that made her happier at the academy. Out of gratitude to her pyrus for helping her improve, Legacy had started to squirrel away endurance bars from the cafeteria. Before practice in the mornings, when it was still dark, she carried them out to the stable.

She had learned to approach her pyrus by taking the same pose she'd used on that first day: forehead down, arm over her head. If she did that, he calmed, and she could get him to eat bits of endurance bar out of her palm.

The increased rations must have been good for his coat, because his coat had gotten shaggier. The pyrus's pink wings turned velvety, and his ribs didn't stick out so much. By the end of the second week, his eyes weren't as red. They had faded to a dark, gentle brown.

Sometimes, when Legacy had trouble sleeping, she snuck out to the stable. She took off her pyrus's collar and his shackles and sat beside him in the hay, keeping him company. She told him about the littles, and Van, and how the stone facade of the orphanage glowed golden when the sun was rising over the Forest of Cora, casting a pink light over the olive trees in the valley. While she talked, he watched her with his big brown eyes. It almost seemed as if he understood every word she was saying.

On the first day of her third week, with only one week left to go before the qualifiers began, Legacy named him Gus. By then, when she entered the barn and called his name, he came to the metal grates of his stall. His snout poked between the bars so that she could scratch his soft, hairy chin or pat his jaw, big and round as one of the dinner plates in the cafeteria.

That was also the day that Javi decided to add a lural to Legacy's training regime. In addition to their secret nightly training programs, he inserted an extra session of interval training into Legacy's daily schedule, during which he loosed the lural—its sinewy muscles rippling, its fangs bared, its spotted coat gleaming in the afternoon sunlight—on Legacy's heels.

Running with a lural behind her was terrifying. Her heart started pounding as soon as Javi led the creature out of the stable, his tug on its harness causing it to emit an occasional howl. It was then that Legacy learned to run not just for the sheer joy of flying—as she did when she was harnessed into the kite—but also as though a creature with bared fangs were running behind her. With three days left to go before the qualifiers began, when Polroy had the kids run sprints in the morning,

Legacy often felt herself pulling ahead, leaving the other kids to catch up.

She had also gotten used to her academy clothes. She still hadn't figured out how to braid, but she'd learned to pull her hair back into such a tight ponytail that it stretched the skin at her temples. It gave her the occasional headache, but at least from the front it vaguely resembled the other kids' styles. And while her new racket continued to vibrate, she grew accustomed to that feeling as well.

The biggest remaining problem was that the qualifiers were only three days away, and she still had no idea how to summon her grana.

As a result, grana class was the worst part of Legacy's day. Every afternoon, after afternoon matches, she and the other qualies showed up to the old classroom full of glass vials, rubber balloons, and enormous contraptions composed of brass scales and bright silver needles.

The class was taught by Argenti, an old man who walked with a cane and spent most of the period standing by the window, scowling and stroking his waxed mustache in a way that made Legacy nervous. His skin was so dry and lined that it seemed to be made of thin paper, but his eyes were sharp. He seemed to notice everything and to find everything—especially if it had to do with Legacy—monumentally disappointing.

From the beginning of her time at the academy, Legacy had deduced that he hated her. While he encouraged all the other students, he only ever seemed to criticize her. Often, she felt him watching her when she worked, as though waiting for her to make a mistake as she performed her exercises.

Most days, these exercises involved Legacy and the other students sitting at their desks, staring at glass spheres that resembled large snow globes. These—as Argenti had instructed his pupils—were called

94

"emotional environments." Each kid's environment was a little bit different. One of Villy's crew, for instance, had an environment that looked like a fancy kitchen. Inside his globe, there was a fireplace, a gleaming pot on a spit, rich tapestries draped over the windows, and a big shining chandelier on the ceiling. One of Gia's crew had a globe full of miniature villas lining the river. The rabbity boy with big glasses had a scene of the Butchers' Bridge, and the almost invisibly thin girl had what looked like a study, with telescopes facing out the window.

Legacy's environment was simpler than that. All she could see in her globe was a hillside, with tiny olive trees on the lower slope and a dark forest stretching up to the ridge. And the air within her globe seemed to be dusky, as though the hillside were waiting for the sun to come up.

It was as if Argenti had designed an environment for Legacy that would remind everyone in grana class that she was different. That she was the only one at the academy who didn't come from the city. As soon as he presented it to Legacy, the other kids started snickering. And Argenti looked down at her with that scowl that reminded Legacy she was on thin ice.

During class, under Argenti's instruction, Legacy and the other kids practiced manipulating their environments. While Argenti showered them with confusing information about the ancient names for minerals and atmospheric conditions, and tossed out incomprehensible phrases like "affect visualization" and "actualized vision," the actual process of changing the weather inside the big snow globes seemed to have very little to do with any of that.

Instead, it seemed to involve glaring at the glass globes until— somehow—the atmosphere within them started to shift.

One afternoon, for instance, the kid from Villy's crew furrowed his brow and focused so hard on his environment that he caused the clouds to grow darker and the wind to pick up until the miniature chandelier started trembling. The pot began to swing on its spit.

Then Argenti cracked a rare smile.

"Well done, my boy, well done!" he said. The boy kept glaring at his globe, and the wind within it kept picking up, until the little round table shook and the porcelain dishes that had been stacked on top slid off and cracked. Argenti continued offering encouragement until, finally, the whole environment shattered.

Everyone in class applauded, and Argenti was so overcome that he flourished his cane in the air. And when he regained his composure, he shot a dark look in Legacy's direction. Because of course she, unlike the other kids, still hadn't managed to summon even the slightest proof of her grana.

All class, she listened carefully to Argenti's confusing instructions about entering states of "relaxed intensity," or using a "sharpened soft gaze." She did her best to obey him. She stared sharply and softly at her environment. She furrowed her brow like everyone else. She narrowed her eyes and glared until her temples ached and the muscles in her jaw twitched.

But still, nothing happened. Her environment remained as quiet and dusky as it had been when Argenti first set it down on her desk.

Sometimes, Argenti hovered behind her. "Don't think so much," he'd say, in a tone that was much harsher than the one he used for the other kids. "You're thinking so much you're not letting yourself feel."

And then Legacy would start thinking about what she was feeling. Then she'd wonder what the difference was, really, between thinking and feeling, until her thoughts and her feelings were such a muddle that the whole process began to seem hopeless.

Then Argenti's voice would become even harsher. "*Feel* it," he'd say. "Feel whatever it is that's building inside you."

And Legacy tried, but all she could bring herself to feel in those moments was anxiety that Argenti would persuade Silla to cancel her scholarship. And meanwhile, her environment remained unchanged on her desk until Argenti finally sighed in audible disappointment and moved off to his usual place by the window.

Sometimes, after class, kids stayed behind to ask Argenti questions. Then, ashamed of her performance, Legacy generally tried to slip out without catching Argenti's attention. Even so, she sometimes felt him watching her as she left. Once, Legacy slipped out so quickly she forgot her grana textbook. When she came back a few minutes later, she saw Argenti standing at the window. A cat had leaped up on the sill, and it was hissing at Argenti.

And Argenti was hissing back at the cat.

Legacy froze. In shock, she stayed very still in the doorway. Suddenly Argenti swung his cane at the cat, and the cat leaped out the window

Before Argenti could see her in the doorway, Legacy ran toward the cafeteria, leaving her book in the classroom.

After that, when the other kids passed her in the hall and made jokes about provis, Legacy remembered that hissing cat. She and that cat had something in common, she thought. They were both Silla's charity projects, unwelcome among the more privileged academy students.

Three days before the qualifiers began, Legacy returned to her room after dinner, shut the door, and—as she had done many nights since she arrived at the academy—tried to summon her grana.

Back on that first day in the cafeteria, Javi had said that she glowed. So Legacy made a nightly practice of sitting on her bed in the dark and trying to imagine a light spreading out from her body.

But as soon as Legacy felt as though maybe something was happening—that her fingertips were starting to warm, or that the roots of her hair might be tingling—she felt herself go cold with fear.

Then she remembered that branch falling on Van. She saw him trapped underneath it, struggling to get out.

They'd been fighting before the branch fell. She'd been so angry. He'd told Legacy that her mother was a witch, and hearing that, Legacy's skin had turned hot. The hairs on her arm had stood up. She'd glared at him and wished he would die, and he kept repeating that her mother was a witch until a sudden flash of light had blinded Legacy. The next thing she saw was a branch falling from a nearby cycapress tree, trapping Van underneath it.

Sitting in her room at the palace, remembering that, Legacy felt as though she'd stepped into icy cold water. Now there was no chance of summoning any grana. All she could think was that she was a terrible person who had wanted to kill her best friend.

She almost *had* killed her best friend. And now she owed it to him to win the nationals, to make up for how badly she'd hurt him.

But the more determined she felt, the more nervous she became. She sat alone in her room, trembling with fear and frustration, until she heard the sound of Pippa knocking, coming to bother her about stringbinds and waxes.

This was their nightly routine: for hours, Pippa would sit on Legacy's bed, her velvet-lined box open wide and little silver corkscrews strewn over the bedspread, running tests on Legacy's racket to see if they could get Legacy to summon her grana.

First Pippa would tighten a horizontal string. Then she'd tell Legacy to hold the Tempest and close her eyes and imagine something that made her afraid. Or she'd tighten a vertical string, then tell Legacy to hold the Tempest and close her eyes and imagine something she dreamed would come true. Over and over again, Pippa fiddled with various strings and tried to get Legacy to channel a feeling. But no matter which tests Pippa ran, nothing happened.

And tonight—three nights before the qualifiers began—was no different than any other occasion. Legacy couldn't summon her grana. Then Pippa arrived and tried to help. But as the hours went by, Pippa became more and more agitated. She was certain that she was missing something.

Sitting beside Legacy on the bed, she moaned in frustration. "How did you tame that pyrus, anyway?" she asked. "Didn't you summon your grana to do that?"

"I just said a chant," Legacy said.

Pippa's eyebrows shot up. "A *chant*?"

"A chant," Legacy said. "A weird little spell. I learned it from a book."

"Which book?"

"This one." Legacy pulled *The Book of Muse* out of her drawer. But when she showed it to Pippa, she realized that even its cover had faded. She could no longer see the gold leaf that had once been embroidered under the title. Now it just looked like a blank notebook.

Embarrassed, Legacy made a motion as if to shove it back into her drawer, but before she could do that, Pippa grabbed it. She flipped through a few pages.

"But . . . it's blank," she said. "There's nothing in here." Then she looked at Legacy with suspicion.

Legacy snatched the book back. "Look," she said. "I know it seems empty. But it wasn't always like that. For some reason it's faded, but there used to be a spell for avoiding scorched eyebrows. There was a diagram, also. A diagram for a proper pyrus mount. You're supposed to get down on your knees and touch your forehead to the ground. That way the pyrus will let you ride on its back."

"Sure, sure," Pippa said in an excessively calm tone of voice. "I'm sure the pages just faded."

For a while longer, Legacy tried to explain the fading pages to Pippa, and Pippa responded in a more and more soothing tone of voice. But the calmer Pippa's voice got, the more annoyed Legacy felt, until finally she stood up.

"Fine," she said. "I'll show you. Unless you're too scared to come with me."

Pippa glared at her for a moment. Then, blowing air out through her lips, she stood and dusted off her wide-legged pants and followed Legacy out to the barn. When she reached Gus's stall, Legacy pushed open the door. Pippa remained in the doorway while Legacy knelt before Gus, placed her forehead in the hay, and covered her head with one arm.

When Gus's front legs buckled so that he could kneel also, Legacy took a deep breath for courage. Then she stood. She stroked the white blaze on his nose and rubbed the shaggy gray fur on his neck. Then, finally, she climbed on his back, sitting down between his pink wings.

"Oh man," Pippa said, still clinging to the door. "Oh man, oh man. You're sitting on top of a pyrus."

Legacy grinned. "Hop on," she said. "We're going out for a ride."

Gus carried them out of the barn. Then they were galloping over the courts and peeling away from the ground and flying up over the palace.

Legacy whooped. Underneath her, she felt Gus's muscles churning while he picked up speed, and they swerved and plummeted around the spires and rooftops of the city, through narrow alleys, up again over gold domes, over stone statues of old champions jutting over the rooftops, over weather vanes shaped like crossed rackets.

This, Legacy thought, was like running around the court on a good day, but faster. Freer, and wilder. From above, the city was more beautiful even than it was on the ground. The domes gleamed. The winding streets unfurled in elaborate patterns. The Tapestry of Granity undulated in the wind. Lights shone on the river; the lanterns in people's windows flickered and one by one winked out for the night. Then Pippa and Legacy and Gus were alone under the reeling stars overhead.

When Gus leveled and starting circling, Legacy looked down to see that the city had shrunk beneath them. It looked like a toy city. Like a city in a globe, an environment contained in a glass vessel.

From this far up, Legacy could make out the villas lining the river. Beyond the city walls, she could see the provinces stretching off into the distance. There were the gashed hillsides of Minori, and the slopes of Agricio, and the dark swath of the Forest of Cora.

Beneath her, Gus's body felt warm. His wings whooshed, and Pippa gripped Legacy's waist. Every so often she let out a whoop to echo Legacy's. They were free, Legacy realized. They could go anywhere they wanted. Legacy was beaming uncontrollably when Gus finally circled back toward the palace and landed on the ledge of the elevated platform that supported the enormous towering board over which the Tapestry of Granity had been stretched.

He knelt. Legacy and Pippa climbed off. The city sprawled below them, and the tapestry towered above them. Its threads gleamed in the dark. The long table seemed to stretch forever. Silla's rust-red robes rippled and flowed in every direction.

Legacy was breathing hard when she sat with Pippa on the edge of the platform, looking down at the city. "That's the river!" Pippa said, pointing. "And that's the villa where my family lives!"

For a moment, a shadow crossed Legacy's heart. The feeling of freedom that had been racing through her veins felt suddenly cramped.

Of course, she thought: of *course* Pippa would choose this particular moment to remind Legacy that she'd grown up in a villa.

But then Legacy looked over at Pippa and saw that her face was miserable.

"I haven't been back there since I came to the academy," Pippa was saying. "I haven't seen my mom for so long."

"She doesn't visit you at the academy?" Legacy said.

Pippa shook her head. "My father won't let her."

Then Legacy remembered the look of irritation on Lucco's face when Pippa and Legacy had matched. She bit her tongue and let Pippa keep talking.

"He was angry that I came in the first place," Pippa said. "He doesn't think I have what it takes. And then I didn't match. For years, I didn't match. All that time, I thought I'd finally prove to him that I was a good stringer as soon as I matched with a player. But now that I've matched with you, he's even more dismissive. He thinks I should give up. He says I'm not cut out to carry on the family tradition. And maybe I *should* stop. I can't even figure out what's wrong with your strings. But what else can I do? I've been at the academy so long, I don't even know my little brother. I can't remember the sound of my mother's voice. I hardly even remember the villa."

"But Javi said you always talk about your happy memories!"

Pippa looked down at her hands. "I made them up," she said in a small voice. "It made me feel better."

"You made them up?" Legacy said.

Pippa nodded. "At least that way I had *something* to think about when I was sitting alone in the cafeteria. Something other than the fact that I hadn't matched yet. Or that all the other kids hate me."

"Oh, Pippa," Legacy said. She leaned forward and gave Pippa a hug. Pippa clutched her back fiercely.

"I haven't been very nice, have I?" Legacy said. "It's just—I thought you'd had it so easy. I thought everyone at the academy had it so easy, compared to what I came from."

"What was it like?" Pippa said. She gazed hopefully at Legacy. "Growing up in the provinces?"

"Oh, I don't know," Legacy said. But before she knew it, she was telling Pippa all about the littles, and Ink's plays, and the olive trees and the Forest of Cora, and how the morning light shone pink on the stone wall. She explained how one of the goats had run off, and how she and the littles often went hungry but how they'd told stories to distract themselves from their hunger. Describing Ink's cape, and her plays, and the way Hugo helped her comb Zaza's hair, she felt a warmth kindle in her stomach, and she realized how proud she was of the way she'd grown up. She and her father and Van and the littles had been a good family, a better family than many of the ones she'd heard about at the academy. Then Legacy felt a pang of guilt about having left them, and she found herself telling Pippa about how she'd wanted to save Van from working in the factories, and how, as a result, she'd

103

disobeyed her own father. How she'd snuck out in the morning before the littles were awake and left them just like her own mother had left her.

Pippa hugged her again. "You'll do it," Pippa said. "I'm sure of it. You'll win the nationals, and you'll save Van."

Legacy glanced up at the tapestry. There was Silla in her robe, her dark hair beaded, her wrists encircled with gold, holding a thunderbolt as a symbol of her grana. She thought about how hard Pippa had worked with her little corkscrews and nail clippers, trying to wind her strings so that she could express her own grana. Then she squeezed Pippa's hand.

"Well, one thing at least is for sure," she said. "I won't be able to win them without you."

CHAPTER TEN

THE GARDEN
OF FEARS

The following night, after another frustrating day in grana class, Javi and Pippa showed up at Legacy's door.

"We have a plan," Javi said. "Also, why are there so many cats in your room?"

Legacy shrugged. She'd gotten used to the cats. They came in the window and found warm corners, where they curled up, watched her, and licked their paws.

"This cat thing has gotten out of control," Pippa said, shooing an orange tabby off Legacy's chair so she could sit down. "It was a nice gesture on Silla's part, but this is just preposterous."

"Could we focus on the plan?" Legacy said. The qualifiers began the day after tomorrow, and she was hoping the "plan" involved something miraculous that would allow her to start summoning grana.

"Follow us," Javi said.

Obediently, Legacy trailed Pippa and Javi while they ascended the stone stairs to the upper floors of the palace. The chandeliers that usually lit the corridors had been put out for the night, but Javi had a torch that he held before them as they climbed. Legacy followed its glow, placing her feet carefully on the softened stones. When they reached the locked door of the forbidden top floor, Pippa fumbled around for a key.

"But it's forbidden," Legacy said. "How—"

"I took the key from my father," Pippa said, coloring slightly under her freckles. "I know it's stealing, and stealing is bad. But it's just for one night. And we won't even look in the workshop."

But Legacy was already shaking her head. "I'm here on a scholarship," she said. "I'm not breaking any rules."

"Don't be an idiot," Javi said. "You think anyone else here is following rules?"

Legacy started to say that everyone *did* seem to be following rules, rules she'd never been taught, but Pippa stopped her by touching her arm.

"What about the pyruses?" she said. "What about the lurals? They're illegal in the rest of the country."

"But—"

"No buts," Javi said.

Then Pippa swung the door open, and Legacy followed the glow of Javi's torch until, in a dark corridor, Javi suddenly stopped and blew it out.

In a moment, the darkness became so complete it felt thick. It felt too thick to breathe, as though the air were wet wool.

Legacy felt her heart beating harder in her chest. "Why did you do that?" she whispered. "What if we can't find our way out? What if we get caught and—"

"You have to light the way," Javi said.

"This is the plan," Pippa said.

Javi nodded. "Now you have to summon your light."

Legacy started to sweat. Every time she tried to breathe, the wet wool got caught in her throat.

"Why would I be able to do it here if I can't even do it in the grana classroom?" Legacy said. Then she felt something warm and soft brush past her ankles. She started—then heard the soft footfall of a cat's paws.

"Because you're afraid," Javi said.

"Because you have to," Pippa said.

"That's what they teach us here at the academy," Javi said. "You'd learn it, too, if you had the benefit of a few extra months."

"But unfortunately," Pippa said, "you don't have a few months. We need you to do this right now."

"Ever wonder why Polroy tells you to run for your life?" Javi said. "Ever wonder why he tells you to play as if your life's on the line? The greatest players play well because they're afraid of what might happen if they don't. They play well because if they fail, they'll lose everything that makes them themselves. Because all they are is champions. If they lose, they're nothing, not even themselves."

"They're nothing more than a dark corridor," Pippa chimed in.

"They're an empty space," Javi said.

"They're—"

"I get it!" Legacy said.

She was still having trouble breathing, but she closed her eyes. She tried to focus. She tried to think about light. She imagined her body glowing. She tried in her mind's eye to see the light's pale fingers creeping along the dark hallway.

"You can do it," Pippa whispered. She was trying to sound encouraging, but a new anxiety had crept into her voice.

"Hurry up," Javi said. Even he sounded worried.

Legacy squeezed her eyes shut even tighter. She tried to focus harder, she tried to imagine a glow beginning to emanate from her skin, but all she could think about was how Javi's breathing had gotten quicker and that Pippa was nervously biting her nails.

"I can't," Legacy said, and she was about to explain, but it was then that they heard a door slam, followed by the sound of human footsteps approaching.

"This way!" Pippa whispered, pushing Legacy into a door that gave inward. At the last minute, Legacy grabbed Javi and pulled him behind her, and they crouched against a wall, huddled together, too afraid of making a sound to shut the door behind them.

Legacy kept her eyes trained on the open doorway. In the faint light from his torch, she could make out Polroy's big, shambling form. She could hear the swishing of his warm-up suit. Then she heard the *tap tap* of Argenti's cane.

"But surely she's shown *some* talent," Polroy was saying.

"None at all," Argenti answered. "She hasn't the least trace of grana."

"I don't believe it," Polroy said. "There's got to be something special about her. Silla wouldn't have chosen her for no reason."

"But there's nothing special in her at all," Argenti said. "She's just another undisciplined provi."

Legacy was glad it was so dark, so nobody could see how she was blinking back tears. Pippa was holding her hand, and even after Argenti's and Polroy's voices receded, Javi kept one finger to his lips until he was sure the instructors weren't coming back.

Then they had to feel their way along the walls of the corridor—following in Polroy and Argenti's wake—to get back to the door that led to the staircase. And by the time they'd climbed back down and made their way back to Legacy's bedroom, she'd had time to compose herself. Then it was Javi and Pippa who seemed more upset.

"What's Argenti's problem?" Javi said.

"Why does he hate you?" Pippa said.

"And how," Javi said, "are you going to learn to summon your grana without him?"

The next night, Pippa and Javi came for her again.

"No," Legacy said, remembering the feeling of the wet darkness clogging her throat, and the warm body of the cat brushing against her leg, and Polroy and Argenti talking about her in the corridor. "No way. Not another big plan."

But Pippa and Javi were insistent. The qualifiers, they reminded her, started tomorrow. And she still hadn't summoned her grana since her first morning at the academy.

Soon enough, Legacy found herself following Pippa and Javi past the courts to the Garden of Fears. In the darkness lit by Javi's torch, Legacy looked around. Boxwood bushes pruned into the shapes of all kinds of animals—pyruses, lurals, and crackles—loomed high overhead. Their gargantuan wings seemed to stretch upward, and their claws raked the air.

They were standing at the base of an enormous bat. Its lifted wings formed a shape like an umbrella split in half. The detail in the pruned limbs was amazing: Legacy could see its catlike ears, the wrinkles in its wings, and the tiny fangs that crept out of its mouth.

Until Javi blew out his torch.

Then he began to "encourage" her once again.

"Why aren't you afraid?" he said. "You should be. You haven't summoned your grana since the first morning here."

"You need your grana to win tomorrow," Pippa said.

"You can't play people like Villy or Gia without any grana," Javi said.

Legacy closed her eyes. She tried hard to feel her fingers warming. She tried to feel a tingling at the roots of her hair. But nothing was happening, and then once again, impossibly, she heard the *tap tap* of Argenti's cane.

"Shh," Pippa said.

The three of them huddled in closer to the bat and peered through the darkness to see the outline of Argenti, hunched over his cane, standing in close conversation with Lucco.

Argenti was saying something and gesturing pointedly with his cane. He was clearly agitated.

"Don't be foolish," Lucco said in response. He said something else, but his voice was too quiet to carry through all the leaves of the garden.

Now Argenti raised his voice. "It will come back to haunt you!" he said, and swung his cane overhead, jabbing it toward the ramparts of the palace. Just then Legacy felt the air stirring around her, and she realized that the enormous bat was flapping its wings.

It was Pippa who yelped. Javi clapped a hand over her mouth, but Argenti and Lucco had already spun around.

"Who's there?" Argenti called.

Lucco reached for Argenti's arm, as if to restrain him. "Leave it," he said. "The bushes are coming to life."

But Argenti pulled his arm free and began hobbling toward Legacy and Javi and Pippa, waving his cane so that the bat flapped its wings even harder. Legacy, Pippa, and Javi took off, sprinting through the Garden of Fears, past a high row of hedges. Then they threw themselves through a gate that opened into a more impenetrable darkness and ran along a silent corridor that smelled of earth and green leaves. For a while, all Legacy could hear was the sound of her heart beating in her own ears. But after a few minutes, she realized that she could no longer hear the sound of Argenti's cane.

Only then did she realize they'd entered the hedge maze.

Then she stopped running, and besides the sounds of Pippa and Javi panting alongside her, she couldn't hear anything at all. Not Lucco's voice. Not wings flapping. Not even leaves stirring in the breeze.

"We're stuck," Pippa said. "We'll never get out."

"Don't worry," Javi said. "We just have to retrace our steps."

But half an hour later, after trying over and over to retrace their steps, they only seemed to have stumbled deeper into the hedge maze, which towered so high overhead that it blocked out the light from the moon.

"Please, Legacy," Pippa said. "Please summon your light."

"If we don't get out of here," Javi said, "they'll have to come find us. They'll know we were out after bedtime. They'll know we were spying."

"We'll all get kicked out," Pippa said.

"*Enough!*" Legacy said. "It's not working. No matter how scared I get, I still can't summon my grana."

Javi was silent.

Pippa was silent as well, but she seemed to be thinking. "Maybe she's right," she said to Javi. "Maybe fear doesn't help her. In the old days, in Ancient Stringing Craft—"

Javi smacked his forehead with the palm of his hand. "Now is *not* the time," he said, "for more blather about Ancient Stringing Craft."

"Let her finish," Legacy said.

"In the old days," Pippa repeated, "stringers used to use minerals representing all the different psychological states: fear, but also love and hate, pity and anger. Now we just focus on fear, but maybe Legacy's grana is more closely related to another psychological state."

"I don't know," Javi said, but Pippa was already excited.

"Maybe something you don't let yourself feel," Pippa was saying. "Something you keep bottled up. Anger, for instance. Maybe it's anger."

Javi looked at Legacy, a new interest rising to his face. "Yeah," he said. "Why aren't you angrier about how all the kids here call you provi?"

"Or how everyone bribes the builders," Pippa said, "but you can't, because your father doesn't have any money."

Legacy had curled her hands into fists. She squeezed her eyes shut. That familiar claw was beginning to curl in her stomach.

"Or how Argenti hates you," Javi said.

"Or how Gia treats you," Pippa said.

"Or the conditions in the provinces," Javi said, running a hand over the scar on his neck. "The shantytowns, the mudslides in the mines, the dangers in the factories."

"Or the fact that your father won't let you play tennis," Pippa said. "Or how your mother left you alone to take care of the littles, or—"

Legacy felt her skin getting hot. Her fingertips were burning. Then the roots of her hair started to tingle.

She knew it was working even before she heard Pippa draw in a sharp breath. When she opened her eyes, she saw that a beam of light had stretched down the corridor of the hedge maze, lighting the way to a door cut into the boxwood bush.

"You idiot," Javi was saying. "You idiot!"

But at the same time he was hugging her, and then Pippa joined in as well, and the warmth in Legacy's fingers only grew warmer. She was angry and laughing at once, and still, her light was glowing. She was leading Javi and Pippa through the hedge maze, shining a narrow, brilliant path through the leaves, slipping through the Garden of Fears and back into the palace.

CHAPTER ELEVEN

ANCIENT STRINGING CRAFT

Back in Legacy's room, Legacy and Pippa and Javi were so excited, they couldn't think of going to sleep, so Javi ran down to the cafeteria to sneak out an armload of endurance bars and recovery goo, and the three of them stayed up late running tests on Legacy's grana.

Pippa had Legacy close her eyes and imagine the little Gias laughing at her burlap shift. When Legacy opened her eyes, a warm faint light had spread over the rich tapestries in her bedroom.

Then Javi handed Legacy her Tempest, and they tried the same exercise again. But this time, nothing happened.

Over and over, they repeated the test. But as soon as Legacy was holding her racket, the glow refused to emerge from her body.

"It should be helping you," Pippa said. "Even with the standard stringbind, it should be magnifying your grana."

"Try again," Javi said, so they tried again, and once more, with the Tempest in her hand, Legacy's fingers couldn't get warm. The roots of her hair wouldn't tingle. Instead, she only felt the same faint vibrations moving up her forearm and fizzing around in her elbow.

"Maybe there's something in that book," Pippa said. "The one where you said you read the chant to avoid getting scorched eyebrows."

Legacy took *The Book of Muse* out of her drawer, but it was as empty as ever. "Nothing," she said. "All the writing is gone."

"What's going on with this racket?" Pippa said, snatching the Tempest from Legacy's hand. She plucked the strings a few times. She held the racket to her ear. Then she furrowed her brow.

"I'm telling you," she said, "it *sounds* wrong. It sounds like the balance is off. If I could just see under this wax—"

"Don't," Javi said, his voice suddenly stern. "It's illegal to tamper with the standard wax."

"I know," Pippa said. But her fingernail was already picking at the red wax coating the strings.

"*Don't*," Javi said. "If we get caught doing this, we'll all get kicked out. And you might just go home to your villa, but I'll have to go back to Mino. I'll have to go back to my family."

"Wait a second," Legacy said. "Your family's in Minori?"

Javi rolled his eyes. "You thought you were the only one from the provinces?" he said. He gestured to the scar on his neck. "They don't let thieves or their children stay in the city."

Legacy was about to ask Javi more, but Pippa was still scratching the wax. Now she was staring at the strings in disbelief.

"They're not brown," she said. "They're supposed to be brown."

Legacy looked at the bare section of strings. They were a vibrant rust red.

"That looks like metium," Pippa said. "That looks like pure, unaltered metium."

Javi leaned in. "Isn't the standard stringbind meant to be a compound of all the minerals?"

"Isn't metium the mineral associated with fear?" Legacy said.

Pippa nodded and glanced at Legacy. "If this stringbind is unmixed metium," she said, "no wonder you can't express anger-based grana. This stringbind will only let you express grana based on fear."

"So that's not the standard bind?" Legacy said.

"Someone must have tampered with your racket," Javi said. "Someone must have messed with your stringbind."

"Did you leave it with anyone?" Pippa said. "Did you give it to someone else to look after?"

"No," Legacy said, but as she shook her head, she remembered that tall girl coming up behind her after she'd matched with Pippa.

"Actually," she said, "that day we matched, I left it on the bleachers. And Gia's stringer brought it back to me later, after the ceremony."

"That's it!" Pippa said. "Gia's been afraid of you since Silla said you'd be the one to beat. She must have gotten her stringer to restring your racket."

Javi was shaking his head, pacing the floor of Legacy's bedroom. "But that doesn't make sense," he said. "Gia knows tampering with a racket will get you a term in Epinmo Prison."

"She also knows she wants to win the nationals," Pippa said.

"I don't know," Legacy said, taking Javi's side. "It seems pretty extreme. And anyway, how would Gia's stringer have the materials to weave a new stringbind? How would she get her hands on pure metium threads?"

"I don't know," Pippa said. "But you guys are missing the point. As long as you're using this stringbind, you're not going to be able to express any grana. The qualifiers start tomorrow. Even if you're lucky enough to get through them without expressing any grana at all, you won't stand a chance against the elites."

"She's right," Javi said, stopping in front of Legacy. "You haven't seen elites when they're competing. You've only seen the qualies. The elites can make the wind change. They can make the shadows shift so you can't see the ball. If you're gonna play against that, you need to be able to externalize your own weather."

"But what can we do?" Legacy said.

"We should tell my father," Pippa said. "We should tell him Gia's stringer tampered with your stringbind."

"But you tampered too!" Javi said. "We all tampered! And if you think I'm going to risk my scholarship . . . if you think I'm going to go back to the provinces, you have another think coming."

"But she can't play with this racket!" Pippa said.

"And we can't tell your father until we have proof that Gia and her stringer meddled with Legacy's stringbind."

"And in the meantime," Pippa said, "is she supposed to play with these strings?"

Legacy took a deep breath. "Quiet," she said. "Both of you." She turned to Pippa. "Can you weave a standard stringbind?"

Pippa grew pale. Nervously, she reached out to pet one of the cats on Legacy's windowsill, but it squirmed out of her grasp.

"I think I could," Pippa said. "I'd just need the recipe. And the right materials."

The cat slipped out the window and disappeared. Javi started pacing again. "Didn't your father write the recipe?"

Pippa nodded.

Legacy smiled. "And don't we have the keys to his workshop?"

The workshop was unlike any place Legacy had ever seen. Every wall was lined from floor to ceiling with wooden shelves, and on the shelves stood glass bottles of brightly hued botanical tinctures: raspberry red, iris-petal purple, some sort of murky brown shot through with flecks of orange.

Some of the shelves were cluttered with little porcelain pots of metal powder; others displayed miniature mallets and saws. One shelf was crammed with rough hunks of rock. Some of these had been sliced to reveal rings of sky-blue stone or moss-green ore or fuchsia crystal. A bin held corals that looked like giant brains. There were drawers spilling over with spools of compound mineral threads, labeled *creeping rose, duck tongue, cormorant feather, fish glue.*

On the floor near Legacy's feet, rows of terra-cotta vats contained what appeared to be wax, some red and some clear. On the opposite side of the room were dozens of looms that looked like big wooden torture devices. They featured massive frames of bent wood, silver wires, long wooden spindles, and shuttles like little canoes.

Legacy walked past them, trailing her hand along the corals, the shimmering wires, the heavy loops of silk thread.

"Hurry," Javi said to Pippa. "We don't have all day."

"I'm looking," Pippa said. She was scouring her father's bookshelf.

"All we need is the standard stringbind recipe," Javi said. "And the threads you need to weave it."

Legacy stopped to stare at the tapestries stretched over the looms. She'd heard of wealthy city dwellers beautifying their homes with tapestries like the Tapestry of Granity. And of course her own room at the academy was decorated with several small fabrics, though those didn't appear to be woven with any reflectors. But these tapestries were almost

118

as colossal as the Tapestry of Granity. And why would they be up here in the attic? Wasn't this a stringing workshop? Why would Lucco be spending his time weaving tapestries?

One, for instance, depicted an enormous, multicolored cat. Another revealed a scene of children playing tennis. Though it was only partially woven, it was already massive. It could have covered the entire wall of Legacy's bedroom. In every possible color of thread, it showed the tiered grass courts behind the palace and groups of children sprinting, playing matches, or training with lurals.

"Try his desk," Javi said.

Pippa headed in that direction, but Legacy couldn't tear herself away from the tapestry. The detail was incredible. There was a figure that looked just like Polroy, even down to his swishing rust-red warm-up suit. The fierce-looking girl with a long braid was clearly Gia. To the side of Gia's court stood a very tall girl, wearing the black uniform of the stringers, standing with a slight hunch.

"The recipe's right here!" Pippa said. "Right out in the open!"

Legacy leaned closer to the tapestry. Was that Javi? Yes, unmistakably woven into the fabric was a boy with a pink scar on his neck. Nearby, a short girl who looked just like Pippa waved her hand wildly at a girl with unbraided hair, wearing a burlap shift, and playing with a warped wooden racket. Legacy's mouth dropped open. That was her. That girl in the fabric was *her*.

And later in the tapestry, just before the weave had been abandoned, she saw herself standing at the center of the court, with Silla herself—High Consul Silla, Silla "the Queen"—waving her hand above her head in a sign of victory.

"I've got it!" Pippa said, waving a scrap of paper over her head. She

119

crossed to the wooden drawers and pulled out spools of metallic thread. "A single thread of dominu," she said, checking the recipe, "and some fish glue, and a whole boatload of compound of metium."

Pippa paused. "That's strange," she said. "It's still a lot of metium. And the one mineral that's not in the recipe is corasite."

"Guys, I think we're in this tapestry," Legacy said.

"Isn't that the mineral that resonates with love?" Javi asked.

"Yeah," Pippa said. "But there's none of it in the recipe."

"Pippa, Javi," Legacy said again. "I think we're in this tapestry!"

Javi froze. "Hurry!" he said. "I think I heard footsteps!"

"Just one more second." Pippa pulled a heavy purple book, entitled *Capulan's Encyclopedia of Minerals and Botanicals*, from her father's bookshelf. She hid it inside her black jacket. Then the three of them hustled out of the workshop.

They were winding down an unlit corridor, away from the sound of the footsteps, when a dark shape flung itself before Legacy's face.

Pippa yelped. A hissing sound split the darkness. And before Legacy knew what she was doing, she was sprinting in the opposite direction. All she could hear were the heavy footfalls of Pippa and Javi running behind her, and they only stopped when they'd ducked into a small, empty room and slammed the door behind them.

"What *was* that?" Pippa said.

"It sounded like a cat," Legacy said.

"If that was a cat," Javi said, "it must be the biggest cat on the planet."

Legacy was about to agree when she heard the familiar sound of balls pinging on strings. They seemed to be coming from inside a little window on the back wall of the room they'd ducked into.

Standing on her tiptoes, peering through the window, Legacy could see a cavernous room full of indoor courts. Polroy sat on the bleachers in his warm-up suit. A few stringers, including the tall girl with the hunch, huddled nearby. And there were the elites. Four of them stood near Polroy, and two were on court.

Villy Sal was playing against Sondra. Villy was clearly winning, pinning Sondra to the baseline. As Legacy watched, pale threatening clouds descended from the vaulted ceiling of the room. Snow began swirling down on Sondra's side of the court. It fell harder and harder, eddying in white torrents.

Villy threw his weight into his shots. He pumped his fist and shouted to himself between points, while snow piled up around Sondra. Soon she was heaving her feet out of drifts between points. She had to run through mounds of snow that came up to her ankles, then her knees, and finally her waist.

"He's doing that," Legacy said, "with his *mind*?"

Pippa and Javi peered over her shoulder in silence.

"I can't compete against that," Legacy said.

"There's no way," Pippa said, "he's playing with the standard stringbind."

Javi whistled. "Who knew?" he said, watching Polroy rise and give Villy a high five. "Ancient Stringing Craft is alive and well in the palace."

CHAPTER TWELVE

A CHILL IN THE AIR

The day of Legacy's first qualifying match, Pippa came to her room in the morning. They hadn't gotten more than a few hours of sleep the night before, but Legacy's nerves about the upcoming match kept her from feeling too tired. She'd have to win today, and again in a second qualifying round tomorrow afternoon, if she was going to enter the nationals and play against the elites.

Pippa must have felt similarly energized, because she chattered away as loquaciously as usual while she helped Legacy choose an outfit from among her new clothes: a rust-red dress with long sleeves and a diamond shape cut out of the back.

"What about paint?" Pippa said.

Legacy grimaced. "What about it?"

"You need a look," Pippa said. "It helps get the crowd on your side."

Legacy thought for a moment.

"Gia does the two stripes on her cheeks," Pippa was saying, "and Sondra does that jagged line down her face. Villy does his eyebrows, and—"

Legacy tried to imagine something that would make her look like the other kids but also a little unique. She felt like she was in grana class all over again, trying to enter a "state of relaxed intensity" or use a "sharpened soft gaze." Finally, she gave up.

"Maybe red stripes on my cheeks?" she said.

Pippa opened her velvet-lined box to a second tier, which contained a little palette of paint and small brushes, and applied Legacy's paint. Then she worked on Legacy's hair, pulling it back so tightly Legacy's temples ached, and parting it three times, in order to weave three braids down her neck.

When she was finished, Legacy looked at herself in the mirror. She looked like an academy player: sleek, professional, and tough. She looked like someone her old self at the orphanage would read about in the *Nova Times*, looking over Van's shoulder.

For a moment, she felt a twinge of homesickness. But she reminded herself that she was here to keep her old life at the orphanage from getting destroyed. Then she picked up her Tempest. Its new strings—woven the night before according to the recipe Pippa found on her father's desk—were freshly coated in red wax.

She heaved it over her shoulder like a battle-ax and headed outside to play her first match.

———

For the qualifying tournament, the higher tiers of courts had been covered in chairs. For the most part, they were full of city people: Legacy could see their rich silks, their braids. Many of them were waving little knockoff tapestries depicting the faces of their favorite players on shiny fabric. Legacy scanned the crowd: not a single flag showed her face.

But on the highest courts, so far away Legacy could barely see the features of their faces, she spotted a few provis in burlap. They must have somehow found a way to get a day off work, and to have their papers signed so that they'd be allowed through the checkpoints at the city gates.

On either side of the main court, two platforms had been erected. One was enclosed in glass. There sat Silla, with her red silks and her gold-beaded braids. She had seated Polroy, Argenti, and Lucco beside her. Behind them were the other senators that Legacy recognized from the Tapestry of Granity.

On the other platform, the two announcers Legacy had met at the provincial championships were seated in high chairs.

"I'm Paula Verini," the woman was saying into a loudspeaker. She was wearing fuchsia silks, and her trademark knotted braids were more complicated than usual.

Angelo smiled a blurry smile. "And I'm Angelo Ditti," he said, then took a swig of whatever liquid he had in his flask and belched into his loudspeaker. Laughter spread through the lower tiers of the crowd when Paula rolled her eyes dramatically, and Angelo slammed his flask down on the desk. This was clearly an act the two of them had perfected.

"Here we have Nina Abrucci," Paula was saying as Legacy's opponent—not one of the strongest qualifiers, but certainly one of the meaner little Gias—made her way onto the court, swinging her braid and smiling up at the crowd.

"Nina's the youngest of the Abruccis," Paula was saying, "and possibly the prettiest."

City dwellers were clapping and shouting. Legacy swallowed and urged herself forward. But as she made her way on court, the clapping suddenly ceased.

124

"And here we have Legacy Petrin," Paula said. "Our little scholarship student."

Angelo took another sip from his flask and leaned toward the loudspeaker.

"Our provincial champion," he said. Paula shot him an odd look. The crowd went silent.

"I see she's taken to wearing stripes on her cheeks," Paula said. "How sweet. A provi trying to look more like Gia."

Legacy's cheeks burned. Trying to calm herself, she bounced the ball twice on the service line. She realized that her hands were trembling. She'd never played before such a big crowd. She hadn't known how nervous she'd get.

She also hadn't realized that the other qualifiers might be hiding their grana. Nina had never expressed much inner weather, especially outside the grana classroom. Legacy had believed that she hadn't developed it either. But now, as Legacy tossed the ball to serve, she felt the air around her getting colder. And when Nina returned the first serve, the air grew colder still.

The better Nina played, the more frigid it became on Legacy's side of the court. Soon, her fingers on the grip of her racket were red. She had to blow on them between points to keep them from freezing.

She knew it was time for her to summon her grana as well. But Nina's grana had unsettled her, and now she was on the defensive. She was afraid she wouldn't be able to summon her grana in these conditions. It was hard to channel her anger when she was on her heels, struggling to keep up with her ground strokes.

She tried to focus on her fundamentals. She'd been beating Nina every day in practice using those. But now her accuracy was off. She was taking the ball late, maybe because her legs were so cold that it was hard to get them moving. And every time she lost a point, the crowd went wild, which sent another chill through her body.

They didn't want her to win, she realized. They wanted her to lose and go home.

Her freezing hand gripped her racket tighter. And when she won the next point, her fingers were warmer. The roots of her hair tingled, and on the announcers' platform, Angelo leaned into his loudspeaker.

"A light grana!" he said in a somewhat slurry voice. "We haven't seen one of these in years!"

"That's pretty neat," Paula said, in a less enthusiastic tone.

But it didn't matter. Legacy's light had gotten so warm that the last of Nina's cold dispersed, and Legacy was moving more quickly now, throwing her weight into each shot. She won that game and the next three after that, but as her light glowed stronger, something strange started to happen.

Sometimes everything felt right, and as her light shone, she played with a power and an accuracy she hadn't had before, even in her best days of practice.

But in other moments, her fingers felt so hot that it was hard to keep her grip on the racket. Then it seemed as though instead of emerging from her body, her light was shooting back up her arm, sending searing pain through her shoulders.

"It's impressive, of course," Paula said into her loudspeaker, "but she doesn't seem to have it under control. It's a little unpredictable. Which, of course, is a behavior trait we've come to expect from our provis."

Legacy paused before serving again. She looked up at the announcers' platform. Was that what city people thought of the provis? That they were unpredictable?

When she glanced back out at the crowd, she thought she saw them jeering. Was that why they'd built that wall, to keep the unpredictable provis from coming into the city? And was that why Gia and her stringer had tampered with her strings, to get the unpredictable provi to lose?

Legacy glanced up at Silla in her enclosed box. Argenti was beside her, looking smug and disapproving. And Polroy on the other side. At one point, Legacy had believed that Polroy was on her side. But now she'd seen him on those secret courts. She'd seen him coaching the elites, with their amplified rackets. That's what everyone at the academy did: trained with pyruses, raced against lurals, tampered with their rackets, all using illegal measures to make sure they were better-off than people from the provinces.

Silla, Legacy realized, was the only one who wanted Legacy to qualify. She'd invited her, after all. She'd given her that scholarship. She was the only one who wanted Legacy to have a chance at winning the championships.

Legacy's body flooded with frustration. The claw of anger raked her stomach. Her fingers burned, but instead of moving out through her racket, the energy shot back up her arm. The pain was so bad that she dropped her racket.

"This is just the kind of temper tantrum you'd expect to see from a provi," Paula said into the loudspeaker.

But it wasn't just temper, Legacy thought while she moved to the other service box. Something was still wrong with her racket.

The heat in her body wasn't moving outward or pouring into her shots. Her fingers burned on the grip, and Legacy lost two more games before she forced herself to close her eyes.

127

Sitting on her bench between games, with her eyes closed, in the darkness, she knew she had to stop using her grana.

She knew she could beat Nina, even without any showy displays. She just had to play with the accuracy and power she'd developed from mornings playing against Gus.

Legacy took a deep breath. And another. She visualized the wall outside the orphanage. She imagined herself playing against it. She heard the *plonk* of the ball bouncing on stone. She heard the *ping* of it striking her racket.

Her fingers cooled. The roots of her hair stopped tingling.

She played the last three games of the match without summoning any grana at all. She kept her emotions flat. She refused to respond when the crowd roared. When the occasional pain shot up through her arm into her shoulder, she only gritted her teeth. She focused again on her technique: the way she lined her shoulders up before swinging; the grip she used on her racket; the number of footsteps she took before lunging into a shot.

Her light dimmed down to nothing. Then Nina's grana began to assert itself again, and it grew very cold on Legacy's side of the court. Still, she clenched her jaw, blew on her numb fingertips between points, and played as though she were practicing against the orphanage wall and it was just an unusually cold morning. Even when she and Nina were in a tiebreaker for the match, she imagined she was playing against a stone wall, and she managed to win the match by a point.

The crowd was strangely silent when she moved up to the net. She shook Nina's hand, and overhead, she heard Paula say: "Not a terrible performance for an unpracticed girl from the provinces."

Pippa and Javi were waiting for Legacy in her room when she came back from the match.

"That wasn't good enough," Javi said.

"You can do better," Pippa said.

Legacy was trembling. "Something's wrong with the strings," she said. She looked at Pippa. "Are you sure you wove the stringbind right?"

Pippa's face went pale. "I'm sure," she said. "I followed the recipe exactly. Compound of metium on the weave, compound of dominu and fish glue on the—"

"It wasn't right," Legacy insisted. "The vibrations were even worse than they used to be. Everything was fizzing up to my elbow."

"That wasn't good enough," Javi said again, as though he hadn't heard her. "Not even for the qualifiers. Definitely not for the elites. Especially now that we know that they're amplifying."

"I *know*," Legacy said, gritting her teeth.

"The other players are definitely amplifying," Pippa said. "I mean, I don't think they're even just using ancient mineral recipes. They're using botanical tinctures in the wax. They're pulling out all the—"

"But something's wrong with this stringbind!" Legacy shouted.

Then, finally, Pippa and Javi fell silent. Pippa's lip was trembling. Javi clasped his hands in his lap, and he seemed to be studying the weave of his fingers.

Immediately Legacy felt a surge of guilt run through her body. She remembered what Pippa had said about missing her mother. Then she glanced at Javi's brand. She thought of everything Javi must have gone through when his family was banished from the city. Then she softened her voice.

"It's not anyone's fault," she said. "But maybe we're in over our heads. Maybe we need to report all this to Lucco. Then he can check my stringbind. He can tell us what to do about the elites."

"But what if he's involved?" Javi said. "I mean, Polroy's involved. And we can assume that Argenti's involved also, since he's been against Legacy from the start. How do we know Lucco isn't in on it also?"

Pippa's lip was still trembling. "My father wouldn't disobey Silla," she said.

"He's our only chance," Legacy said.

"Okay," Javi said. "Assuming you're right. What if he doesn't believe us about Gia's stringer tampering with your racket? Then we're the only ones who've been tampering with the string wax. That's enough to get us expelled."

Legacy glanced at Pippa. "He's your father," she said. "Won't he believe you?"

Pippa looked down. "I don't know," she said in a very small voice. "I don't know if he'd believe me."

"We need proof," Javi said. "Concrete evidence that the elites are messing with Ancient Stringing Craft."

"We know Gia's stringer's involved," Legacy said. "What if we could find something in her room? Ancient Stringing Craft materials? Some botanical tinctures or amplifying wax or whatever minerals she used when she messed with my racket?"

"But how do we get into her room?" Javi said. "Her door will be locked. And her window's on the seventh floor. Unless you guys have some sort of plan to grow wings—"

"Gus!" Pippa said.

"Who's Gus?" Javi said.

Legacy smiled.

They waited until night to get Gus out of the stable. Then, under cover of darkness, Pippa and Legacy climbed on. Only Javi remained on the ground.

"Hop on," Legacy said.

"No way," Javi said. He was shaking his head and slowly backing away.

"What's wrong?" Pippa said.

"Uh-uh," Javi said. "Not in a million years."

Pippa and Legacy glanced at each other. "Are you afraid of flying?" Legacy said.

"No," Javi said, still backing away. "I just—"

Pippa laughed. "The great Javi, number-two-ranked builder in the whole country, tough guy extraordinaire, is afraid of—"

"I'm not afraid of flying!" Javi said. Scowling, he moved toward the pyrus. Then he pressed his eyes shut. Grimacing, he climbed on.

Legacy squeezed Gus with her knees. She whispered in his ear. Then he was galloping, and surging up into the sky, and the only sound Legacy could hear was Javi shouting, "I really, really, really hate flying!"

Javi kept complaining until they were airborne, and only then did he grow quiet. Then Legacy felt his grip on her shoulders loosen. When she turned, she saw that he was gazing below him in wonder.

"It's not so bad," he whispered. "It's actually pretty beautiful."

Using her knees, Legacy guided Gus past the seventh-floor windows. She had him slow as they passed the stringers' rooms. They'd winged by four or five before they saw Gia's tall stringer lying in her bed, reading a book, and Gus paused just long enough for Pippa to spy three glass vials out on her desk, each containing a small amount of jewel-colored liquid.

"Botanical tinctures!" Pippa said. "To taint the string wax!"

"Proof!" Legacy said.

"I feel a little sick to my stomach!" Javi said.

Gus flew them back to the stable, and once Javi got his footing again, and denied for the millionth time that he was scared of flying, they headed back to the palace. On their way up the stairs, the three of them planned their next move.

"Now we go to your father," Legacy said. "We tell him the whole story, and if he doesn't believe us, we take him to Gia's stringer's room."

"How did she even get those vials?" Pippa said. "She must have broken into my father's workshop. But how did she get the key?"

"That doesn't matter," Javi said. "What matters is that it's evidence."

Legacy was watching Pippa's face. She was still unusually pale.

"You're sure your father's not involved with the elites?" Legacy asked.

Pippa shook her head firmly. "He's loyal to Silla," she said. "There's no way he'd betray her."

"Then it's decided," Javi said. He looked at Legacy. "We go to Lucco tomorrow."

"Before my match?" Legacy said.

Pippa bit her lip. "He won't be alone in the workshop until after the matches are finished."

Javi nodded in agreement. "We can't risk confronting him in front of anyone else."

"After my match, then," Legacy said. Then she remembered the shooting pains radiating up into her elbow and grimaced.

"No grana," Pippa said.

"Keep it under wraps," Javi said.

"Sure," Legacy said, and tried to pretend those weren't her nerves jumping up and down in her stomach.

CHAPTER THIRTEEN

CORASITE DUST

In the morning, before Legacy's second and final qualifying match, Pippa helped braid her hair while maintaining a relentless stream of nervous advice.

"You've got to keep your emotions under control," she said, pulling Legacy's hair so tight she winced.

"Got it," Legacy said.

"It's great that you're expressing your anger," she said, painting her cheeks. "But you also have to stay measured and calm. You can't be so intense and dramatic."

"Got it!" Legacy said, standing up from the stool and stepping away from Pippa in irritation.

She looked at herself in the mirror. With the red lines on her cheekbones, her three braids, and her red dress, she looked like any other academy student.

And yet even her own stringer was doubting her ability to keep her emotions under control. And when she went on court, the announcers would doubt it as well. So would the crowd. They'd comment on how she was imitating Gia, but they'd all be watching her more closely than they watched the little Gias. They'd be waiting for her to show her true colors. Waiting for her to express her "unpredict-able emotions."

Outside, as she headed onto the main court, Legacy felt the crowd's eyes on her skin. She felt what they expected from her. She knew how she'd have to behave to persuade them she was worthy. Even if she was the only player here representing the provinces, she would have to remain perfectly calm. Even if her best friend might have to go work in the factories, she couldn't act dramatic or in any way "out of control," because otherwise she'd confirm their opinion that she was an unpre-dictable provi.

Before she even hit the first shot, Legacy's hand on her racket was a clenched fist.

Across the net, her opponent was bouncing the ball, preparing to serve.

"Here we have Robby Groggio, of the silk Groggios, preparing to serve," Paula was saying. "And what a serve he has, a serve we can be proud of!"

Legacy felt the claw in her stomach beginning to reach toward her fingers and up to her skull, tingling the roots of her hair.

Still, she managed to keep her anger under control for the first set. Robby was one of Villy's followers. He had a weak backhand. She'd beaten him in practices before. Now he was causing the winds to buffet around her, but luckily, even though he was physically stronger than Nina, his grana was weaker. His winds weren't much more effective than the normal morning breeze Legacy felt in her hair when she was playing against Gus.

She won the first set without summoning any grana. In the second set, as well, she did everything she could to keep her grana under wraps. She remembered how much it had hurt in her match against Nina, and when she felt her fingertips getting too hot, she closed her eyes and remembered playing against the orphanage wall. Mechanically, she counted her footsteps. She timed her shots. She listened for the *ping* of the ball striking her strings.

For the most part, it worked. She was up in the second set and serving to win the match, when she heard Paula.

"Sure, sure," Paula was saying, "she's playing well for a girl from the provinces. But we can't expect her to hold up in the nationals if she's matched against the elites."

Across the court, she saw Robby snicker. Despite the fact that he was losing, with his stupid Villy pompadour and his weak grana, he was snickering at Legacy.

She drew up short for a moment. Everyone, she thought, was against her. Robby and Paula, Polroy and Argenti. Even Pippa didn't believe in her ability to control her emotions, and Pippa was supposed to be her friend.

At that, the claw in Legacy's stomach started burning. Heat shot toward her fingers. She felt a flash of rage and a moment of perfect confidence that she would be the best player ever to compete in the republic.

As Legacy served, her hand was scorching hot. When her racket struck the ball, a flash of pain shot up her body and ricocheted in her skull.

The whole world started to tilt. The audience in their chairs slid up toward the clouds. Legacy's head hit the ground, and the world went instantly black.

Legacy opened her eyes and looked around. She was lying in a room lined with glass cabinets that were stacked with rolls of athletic tape and boxes of recovery sleeves. In the corner, there was a pool of steaming, roiling, burbling water. She was occupying one of a few narrow cots lining the walls, and Pippa and Javi were sitting beside her.

"Sorry it took so long for us to come," Pippa said.

"Argenti's been guarding the door," Javi said.

"He won't let anyone visit," Pippa said.

"He keeps muttering about cats and spies and plots afoot," Javi said. "The only way we could get him to leave was to tell him there were a ton of cats in your bedroom. Then he rushed off, muttering and waving his cane."

Legacy blinked at them. How long had she been lying here? The last memory she could dredge up was the thump of her head hitting the ground. Before that, she remembered serving. Then her stomach sank. She must have fainted on the last point of the match.

"I lost," she said. She thought of Van. She saw him sitting in the attic, wearing his crooked glasses, his bad leg pulled up underneath him. She'd failed him. She hadn't even made it to the nationals.

"You idiot," Javi said. He was shaking his head and smiling.

Legacy glared at him in dismay. How could he be smiling now?

"You won!" Pippa said. "You beat him."

"But I fainted—"

"Your last serve was an ace," Javi said.

"Then you passed out," Pippa said. "And you've been here since yesterday, and nationals start tomorrow, and we still haven't figured out what to do with your racket."

Now everything began to flood back. Legacy remembered Pippa

braiding her hair before the match and Pippa's warning to keep her emotions in check. Then Legacy's hurt—for Pippa to doubt her, after all that claptrap about players and stringers trusting one another—began to flood back as well.

Pippa must have noticed the shift in Legacy's expression, because her smiled faded as well.

"I'm so sorry, Leg," she said.

"It's Legacy," Legacy murmured.

"It was my fault," Pippa said. "It wasn't your fault at all. That stringbind—the one we found on my father's desk: it could have killed you."

She pulled out her copy of *Capulan's Encyclopedia*.

"Look," she said, gesturing at a page with illustrations of an array of porcelain pots full of various metal powders. "It's all here. A player with light grana—that's you—is corasite-intense. That means you resonate with corasite, the metal associated with love. Even your anger—it resonates with corasite. And to play with a stringbind that doesn't have any corasite is extraordinarily dangerous."

Legacy shook her head. She was remembering that flash of light and the branch falling on Van. "But anger," she said. "How's that associated with love?"

"I don't know exactly," Pippa said.

Legacy thought for a moment. She remembered how Van had called her mother a witch. And in that moment, Legacy had felt love for her mother welling up in her heart. And that love had turned into anger.

"Maybe the source of anger is love?" Legacy said.

"Maybe without any love," Javi said, "your anger has nowhere productive to go."

Legacy and Pippa shot each other a glance. It was a pretty insightful comment, especially coming from Javi. Noticing their surprise, he scowled and crossed his muscled arms over his chest, trying to look as though he hadn't wasted any time contemplating emotions.

"The heat was shooting back up my arm," Legacy said, "into my shoulder."

"Directing inward," Pippa said. "Not outward."

"I was directing my anger at myself?" Legacy said.

Pippa pointed to an illustration of a porcelain pot full of vermilion corasite dust. "Look here," she said, reading from the page. "Corasite resonates not only with love for others, but also with self-love. Both must be permitted to express for anger grana to move in the proper direction. Without expression of self-love, anger grana will redirect inward."

"So without any corasite in her racket," Javi said, "she can't channel any self-love?"

"And without self-love," Pippa said, "her anger moves inward?"

"That's why that stringbind's so dangerous," Javi said. "It redirects all your grana back into your body."

"It could have been fatal," Pippa said. She looked at Legacy. "I could have killed you, just by weaving that stringbind."

"It's not your fault," Legacy said. "You only followed the recipe we found in your father's workshop."

Javi nodded. "She's right," he said. "But that can't be the standard stringbind, right? Could you have grabbed the wrong recipe?"

"But it said 'Recipe for the Standard Stringbind,'" Pippa said.

"Maybe someone planted it there," Javi said.

Legacy shivered. "Maybe someone knew we were coming."

"Someone who wanted you to lose," Javi said.

"Or someone," Pippa said, "who wanted to kill you."

Legacy felt her face go cold. "But who would want to kill me?"

Javi started pacing. Pippa furrowed her brow.

"Do we still report this to your father?" Legacy said.

"I'm not sure that's such a good plan," Javi said. "I mean, we found that recipe on his desk. What if he's the one who planted it there?"

Legacy glanced at Pippa. She was biting her lower lip.

"But what else can we do?" Legacy said.

"I could try to re-string it," Pippa said, her voice wavering.

Javi nodded. "You could try to add some corasite."

Legacy felt a rush of love for her friends. They'd already risked so much on her behalf: tampering with stringbinds, sneaking onto forbidden floors of the palace, flying around at night on winged horses. They were risking their places at the academy. Pippa was risking her relationship with her father. And Javi was risking going back to the provinces. Legacy felt as if her heart couldn't expand any more in her chest.

"Thank you," she said, looking at Pippa, then Javi. "But no. No more secrets. No more sneaking around. I'm not letting you two get kicked out."

"But you can't play with those strings," Pippa said. Javi nodded in agreement.

Legacy shook her head. She remembered that all of this mess had come from disobeying her own father and sneaking around despite rules forbidding such dangerous behavior. Maybe Polroy *was* breaking the law. Maybe Argenti was with him. But that didn't mean no adults could be trusted. Silla, after all, had invited her to the academy. Her father had steadfastly loved her. Sometimes, Legacy thought, it was best to trust adults, who usually understood things more clearly.

"No," she said. "No more sneaking around. No more risks. I've hurt too many friends already. We're going right now to report this to your father."

It was Javi's idea to distract Argenti by making a commotion about cats coming in through the window. Swinging his cane, Argenti came charging into the infirmary, and while he was busy searching for cats, the three of them snuck out. They headed up to the workshop.

On their way down the forbidden corridor, Pippa whispered to Legacy. "What did you mean about hurting too many friends?" she said.

"Always chattering," Javi muttered.

Pippa rolled her eyes. But from then on, she held her tongue. They moved in silence as they headed toward the doorway into the workshop, which was how they were able to hear voices before they'd even rounded the corner.

"It's not right," a girl's voice was saying. "It's not fair."

Legacy froze. Behind her, Javi and Pippa froze also.

"If Gia doesn't win," a man said in response, "Silla won't continue supporting your mother."

There was a long silence. Legacy crept closer to the door, then peeped past the corner. There, in the workshop, Lucco was sitting before the tall girl with the hunch.

He was holding out a pot of wax and a glass bottle of tincture, one in each hand.

Gia's stringer stared at the pot without moving. Her face twisted like a wet dishrag getting wrung out.

"There's only one way to ensure Gia wins," Lucco said.

Still, Gia's stringer hesitated. Lucco pushed the wax and the vial toward her again. Finally, the girl reached out, took them, and rushed for the door.

Legacy, Pippa, and Javi flattened themselves against the stone wall of the corridor. Legacy held her breath. It was only thanks to the darkness in the passageway that Gia's stringer dashed by them without noticing.

Once her footsteps had faded down the corridor, Legacy peered around the doorway again.

Now Lucco stood before the looms. He was facing the tapestry that depicted an enormous multicolored cat. He seemed to be speaking to the woven cat when suddenly a real cat leaped out of the fabric, hissed, and started running straight for the doorway.

With the cat on their heels, Legacy, Pippa, and Javi sprinted for the stairs. They stumbled down them, and ran as fast as they could back toward the infirmary, and they'd just rounded the corner when they collided with Argenti. His face was black with disapproval, and he was holding his cane over his head, as if ready to strike them.

CHAPTER FOURTEEN

THE BOOK
OF MUSE

Stay put," Argenti hissed, and pushed Legacy, Pippa, and Javi into the corner of the infirmary. Then he took a pot of wax from his pocket and sealed the crack under the door. He checked the window, pulled the drapes, and turned back to Legacy and Pippa and Javi.

He sighed. "The lengths I have to go to in order to keep the cats from spying," he said.

Pippa made a small, weird whimpering noise.

"Calm down," Argenti said. "You've had a fright."

Then he sat on a cot and crossed one leg over the other. Red socks peeked out beneath his tweed trousers.

"The cat," Legacy said. "It jumped out of the—"

"The tapestry?" Argenti said.

Legacy nodded.

Argenti sighed again. "Yes. That's one of Lucco's newer tricks. They gather information at the academy, then bring it back to him and Silla. They're not real, of course. They're made of threads."

"But they look like—"

"Yes," Argenti said. "They look like real cats." He turned to Pippa.

143

"Your father's weaving techniques are extraordinarily lifelike."

Javi was staring at Argenti. "But why—"

"To spy on the students," Argenti said.

"They can *talk*?" Javi said.

"I admit that I'm not quite sure how it works," Argenti said. "Obviously these new weaving techniques have been kept very quiet. One thing that is clear, however, is that the cats aren't your typical house pets."

"So let me get this straight," Legacy said. "All the secret conversations we've had in my room, about planning to sneak up to the workshop, or planning to find the recipe for the secret stringbind—all those might have been reported by *cats*?"

"Reported to my father?" Pippa said.

"And—to *Silla*?" Javi said.

Argenti nodded.

Legacy felt her stomach drop. It couldn't be true. Silla couldn't be spying on her. It was Silla, after all, who had set up the provincial trials. Silla who had provided the scholarship that had allowed Legacy to attend the academy. Why would Silla spy on her? She remembered Silla watching her in the provincial trials. She remembered feeling as though Silla had locked eyes with her when she won. She'd believed that Silla believed in her. All this time, she'd imagined that Silla was behind her. All this time, no matter what disturbing events had occurred—a pyrus breathing fire down her neck, a cat slipping under a door, even the elites practicing Ancient Stringing Craft—Legacy had imagined that nothing really disastrous could happen. Not with Silla in charge. Silla the Queen. Silla the greatest champion in the republic, who stopped the Great Fire and united the people. But if Silla was part of a plot that the elites were hatching, a plot involving Ancient Stringing Craft . . . Suddenly the whole quest to win nationals and save Van didn't just seem like a long shot. It was starting to seem like a death wish.

"So it's Silla," Legacy said, in a very small voice, "who's behind all this?"

"And my father?" Pippa said. Her lower lip was trembling.

"Not just him," Argenti said, tapping the floor with his cane for emphasis. "We're all meant to assist her. Me, Lucco, Polroy. We'd be fired if we didn't."

Now he heaved himself up and went to the window. For a moment, he stood in silence, twisting his mustache. He looked even more dismayed than he had during grana class when Legacy couldn't summon her inner weather.

"Of course Polroy's a true believer," he said. "He lost his family's estate in the Great Fire. Now he truly believes that if we're not governed by a ruler like Silla—one who inspires fear in her subjects—we'll fall into disorder again. And your father, Pippa, was a true believer as well. But at this point I've come to suspect that he only follows Silla's bidding to protect his family. I've tried to get through to him a few times, but he's always resisted. He won't risk your safety. Yours, or the safety of your mother, and your siblings at home. That's why he's always kept the rest of them far away from the palace. You're the only one who insisted."

"But why?" Legacy said. "Why would Silla want to bring back Ancient Stringing Craft? Why would she want to spy on her own students and keep me from winning nationals?"

"I wasn't sure either," Argenti said. "At least at first. It seemed to me that her power as high consul was consolidated enough. The people are grateful enough to keep imagining her in the high consul position for decades. Why, then, should she fool around with surveillance

145

techniques? Why break her own dictates? But then I saw you," he said, turning toward Legacy, "and I saw the resemblance."

"Resemblance?" Javi said, peering at Legacy.

Pippa looked also. "Resemblance to whom?"

Legacy felt her face growing hot.

"Why, her resemblance to Amata," Argenti said, furrowing his brow.

"Amata?" Legacy said. The name struck a chord somewhere within her. Then she remembered again sitting in the cart on her way into the city. She was surrounded by chickens and hay, and she was reading the book Van had slipped into her sack.

For Legacy, from Amata

the inscription had read.

Argenti looked down at his hand on his cane. "You didn't know," he said in a quieter voice. Then he paused and turned back to the window. "Well, well. I'm sorry this is how you're finding out."

"Finding out what?" Legacy said.

Argenti turned and tapped the floor with his cane. "That Amata was your mother. And that she was Silla's only sister."

Legacy stared. Her father had only ever told her that he and her mother had started the orphanage a few months before Legacy was born. After three years, her mother left. Legacy had never been told anything about stringing. She'd never been told anything about Silla.

"Amata was Silla's stringer," Argenti went on. "This was back in the early days, when Silla was still a tennis champion. The Great Fire hadn't yet started burning, and she hadn't yet put it out. She hadn't yet appeared in the Tapestry of Granity. She wasn't high consul. She was still the Queen, and your mother wove her stringbinds. Your mother created the binds that allowed her—later—to summon that storm.

"Once Silla was elected," Argenti went on, "she began to experiment with more methods for consolidating her power. Ostensibly, it was to end the violence in the republic started by the senators. She researched ancient techniques for prognosticating tapestries, and she asked Amata to weave one, in order to predict insurrections that might rise up in the future. It had been years since anyone had dared to tempt the gods' wrath by weaving a prognosticating tapestry, but Amata agreed."

Legacy's eyes shot open wider. "The gods?" she said.

Argenti scowled at her. "You didn't think we all just stopped believing overnight?"

Legacy bit her tongue. "Sorry," she said. "Go on."

"Your mother agreed," Argenti continued. "She even started. You can see it still—it's still up on one of the looms in Lucco's workshop. Amata got as far as this academy, and then one day she simply stopped."

Here Argenti tapped the floor with his cane for emphasis. His brows were pulled down low over his eyes, like black beetles. Legacy could see how fatal he believed Amata's decision had been.

"She was pregnant," he said, "at the time. And she wouldn't continue. You can imagine how angry Silla was. It caused a great rift between them. Silla threatened to imprison her, but your mother simply wouldn't sit at the loom. Finally, Silla banished her to the provinces."

"I thought Silla's sister died in the fire," Pippa said.

"That's what she said to the papers," Argenti said. "In fact, no one knew what became of Amata. Somehow she even eluded the crackles."

"The *crackles*?" Javi said.

"Thread crackles," Argenti said, gesturing distractedly with his cane. "Silla's spies in the provinces."

Javi touched the brand on his neck. "That's how she must keep tabs on families like mine," he said.

Argenti sighed. "Yes," he said, looking down and brushing off his tweed pant leg. "A shame about that. But unfortunately, after that incident with the prognosticating tapestry, Silla's punishments for any insurrectionary behavior have become harsher and harsher."

"She was afraid that Amata had seen an uprising?" Pippa said. "The 'insurrectionary behavior' she'd hoped to prevent?"

"Exactly," Argenti said, nodding at Pippa in approval. "She was so afraid that—once she'd put out the Great Fire—she trained your father to continue with the tapestry. But his talents aren't quite at Amata's level. He could only proceed a little longer with the tapestry. Then the threads began to elude him. Still, by the time he finished, Silla had seen enough."

"Something involving Legacy?" Pippa said.

"A girl," Argenti said, "wearing the garb of the provinces. With a face just like her sister's. Directly challenging Silla's power as high consul."

Legacy stood from the cot where she'd been sitting. She walked over to the stacks of athletic tape and began to pick at the edge of one roll with her fingernail to distract herself from the nerves that had begun to brew in her stomach.

"But why?" she said. "Why would I challenge Silla's power? She's the one who put out the Great Fire!"

"At first," Argenti said, "I didn't understand either. But prophecies have a way of fulfilling themselves. The more frightened Silla became of the girl who challenged her authority, the more she provided reason for

148

such a girl to exist. She began spying. She changed the standard string-bind, heightening metium levels. That way, only fearful children—loyal children—could express grana. Those children, whose grana resonates with metium, became more and more successful. They are the champions who each year pledge their loyalty to Silla, reinforcing her power."

"That stringbind," Pippa said, "the one that Legacy started with—it wasn't brown. It was rust red."

"That's the standard now," Argenti said. "Thanks to your father and Silla. Of course, it's a crime. Manipulating children through their stringbinds. Encouraging their fearfulness. Causing them to be unquestioningly loyal. Playing with a stringbind like that changes a child. It not only causes them to express fear, it strengthens their fear reflex. It builds their fear muscle. It alters their most essential selves."

"*A self disguised is a death surmised*," Legacy murmured, remembering the book of Cora stories.

Argenti nodded, surveying Legacy over his pronounced nose with a look that almost resembled approval. "As soon as you showed up at the trials," he said, "and I saw the resemblance to Amata, I knew that Silla had set up your scholarship to lure you into the academy, where she could control you. I knew she'd attempt to manipulate you through your strings. That's why I was so hard on you in grana class. I knew your grana would have to be exceptionally strong if you were going to resist her techniques."

"But in the attic," Legacy said, "we overheard you telling Polroy that I didn't have any grana."

"Even as I saw you improving," Argenti said, "I tried to hide it from the other teachers. To keep them from strengthening their manipulation techniques. But even so—"

149

"That 'standard bind,'" Pippa said. "The one we found on my father's desk. It wasn't standard."

Argenti shook his head. His dark eyes grew even darker. "No," he said.

"There was enough of a mix that Legacy could start to express grana fueled by anger," Pippa said.

"But there wasn't any corasite," Javi said.

"So any grana-fueled anger I summoned," Legacy said, "didn't express outward. It just shot up my arm."

Argenti nodded. "Silla must have decided that just keeping you from expressing wasn't enough."

"She had my father plant a recipe," Pippa said.

"A recipe that could have killed me," Legacy said.

Now Javi stood up. His face had darkened. He was glaring at Argenti.

"And you didn't think you should tell us?" he said. "You knew all this, and you didn't think you should warn us? Legacy could have died playing with that stringbind. We all could have died, flying around on that pyrus, looking for evidence of a crime you knew about all along."

Argenti sighed. "I'm an old man. My position here is tenuous. I knew I couldn't expose Silla alone. I was waiting for Legacy to show up. And, once she did, I was waiting for her to be ready. I wanted her grana to be strong enough to withstand Silla's manipulations. Unfortunately, however, it seems that Silla has chosen now as the moment to act. It appears that she wants to use this tournament to eliminate any possibility of Legacy threatening her domination."

"So that explains it," Pippa whispered.

"It also explains what we saw on those secret courts," Javi said.

"Secret courts?" Argenti said.

"We saw the elites practicing with Polroy," Javi said. "Summoning grana that couldn't have been possible with a standard bind."

"Blizzards," Legacy said. "Waist-high snowdrifts."

For a moment, Argenti rested his head on the handle of his cane. When he looked up again, his face was tired.

"That's what I feared," he said. "But I didn't know. It's been some time since Silla trusted me. I've expressed my dissent one too many times. Once Silla started manipulating the standard stringbind, I knew we were only a step away from amplifying again. Or from allowing some students to amplify, and not allowing others."

"But what do we do?" Legacy said. "How can we stop her?"

"You can't oppose her outright," Argenti said. "The people are all behind her. If you try to speak out now, you'll be banished, and no one will challenge the decision. She's Silla, high consul of Nova. She once put out the Great Fire. She once ended the wars. And you're just an unknown from the provinces."

"And I'm just the child of a thief," Javi said.

"And I'm just a spoiled child of privilege," Pippa said.

Argenti nodded wearily, looking down at his red socks.

"But if she wins the championships," Javi said.

"If she summons more grana than anyone else," Pippa said.

"If she plays better than any champion the country has ever seen," Javi said.

"And if I don't profess loyalty to Silla," Legacy said.

All three of them looked at Argenti.

He pursed his lips. "It's risky," he said. "But I don't see a better approach."

Legacy turned toward Pippa. "Could you weave me a new string-bind?" she said. "One that would allow me to express without danger?"

"I could try," Pippa said.

"*Try?*" Javi said. "You've been talking about Ancient Stringing Craft since I came to the academy!"

"Yes," Pippa said, "but in all the old books, they say to consult the 'ingredient list' for the proper mineral compounds. And I don't know where we find the right 'ingredient list.'"

"In the old days," Argenti said, "before you were born, when Silla was still the Queen and Amata was her head stringer, each child at the academy was given a woven book, threaded with the old techniques. That way the book reflected the player's emotional life. It generated recipes with the particular mineralogy necessary for that particular player. Chants and diagrams, as well. Anything that might help that player find her truest course. Each book could be read only by the child it was intended for, to prevent other players from tampering with the strings. That way, if that child disguised her inner weather too long, or expressed it untruly, she became alienated from her book. We called it a death in life. After that, the book became hard to read. Its pages faded. The threads began to unravel."

"*The Book of Muse,*" Legacy said. She remembered Van's note: *Just thought this might be meant for you.* Then she felt a strange pressure in her chest, as though a flower that had been tightly squeezed shut were beginning to open. It *had* been meant for her, to show her how to become a player who would challenge Silla's domination. Her mother had known. She'd woven it for her. She'd given her that gift before leaving. "*The Book of Muse,* that's what it was!"

Argenti looked at her sharply. "You have one?" he said.

"She must have made me one," Legacy said. "My mother. Before she left—"

"That's it, then!" Javi said. "All we have to do is find the recipe in the book!"

"But it's faded," Legacy said, her heart sinking into her stomach. "I can't read it anymore. I can't even read the inscription—"

"We have to try again," Pippa said. "And this time no disguising yourself."

CHAPTER FIFTEEN

PATCHES OF ICE

*T*he *Book of Muse* was still blank when they pulled it out of Legacy's drawer.

"Wait a second," Legacy said.

She opened her closet and looked at herself in the mirror. She was still wearing the sleek red dress she'd worn in her last match and the red stripes under her eyes. Her hair was still tightly braided.

She took a deep breath. She scrubbed the paint off her face and changed into her burlap shift. Then, one by one, she loosed her braids. She looked at herself in the mirror once again.

Released from the braids, her hair was curlier than ever. When the light struck it, it looked as though she were wearing a halo.

Legacy smiled. She was a little stronger than she used to be. Her shoulders were wider. Her muscles were bigger. Her skin was darker from long days outside, training under the sun. But wearing her burlap, with her paint washed off, her hair loosed from the braids, she almost looked like the same girl she'd been when she hopped on that cart, sat with the chickens, and first read her *Book of Muse*.

Almost the same, but better. Stronger. More beautiful. Herself, but more certain that herself was exactly who she wanted to be.

"*A self disguised is a death surmised,*" she whispered to herself. She remembered sitting in the orphanage, reading those stories to Ink and the littles. She closed her eyes. She saw the moth-eaten tapestries, the tangled weeds in the garden, Van stumbling toward her in the darkness. She inhaled the scent of dust and old books, wild honey and corn cakes.

Then she opened her eyes again. She sat down with Pippa and Javi, and reopened *The Book of Muse.* Van's note fluttered out:

> Just thought this might be meant for you. Think of me when you're famous!
>
> From.
>
> Van

Legacy smiled. She could remember him feeling his way toward the back wall where she was playing tennis, telling her that she was lighting the darkness. Waving the *Nova Times* over his head. Believing that she could be great, even when she herself didn't believe it.

When she folded up the note and looked back at the book, she could see faint colors dotting the pages. It was as though the threads were recalling their old pigments. But the words were still too faint to read.

"Tell us what it was like," Pippa said. "Back at the orphanage. Before you came to the academy."

So Legacy tried. She talked about the olive trees: the way the tops of their leaves were glossy and green and the undersides were soft silver. She talked about the cold tumbled stone underfoot, punching into her arches like fists. She talked about Ink's cape, and the goats in their barn, and how Van milked them in the mornings. She talked about how her father had threatened to send Van to work in the factories, and how she couldn't let that happen. Then she remembered Van's limp. She remembered him tripping on the stairs when he ran away from her in tears. Then she stopped talking.

"Keep going," Pippa said.

"The colors are getting brighter," Javi said.

Legacy took another deep breath. She looked at Pippa and Javi. She didn't want to tell them about how she'd wished Van would die. About what she'd done to him. How could they be her friends after that? How could they support her?

"What?" Pippa said. "What were you going to say?"

"No—nothing," Legacy stammered.

"You idiot!" Javi said. "It's fading!"

"Please," Pippa said. "We can't get your recipe if the writing won't show up."

Legacy squeezed her eyes shut. "His leg," she said. "One of Van's legs was broken so badly it never quite healed. It was my fault. I did it."

Once she'd started, the words kept tumbling out: about how she'd felt such anger, and light had flashed, and the tree branch had fallen. She told them how long Van had lain trapped beneath it. How he'd been at death's door. How once his leg had healed, they never discussed what happened.

By the time she'd finished the story, Legacy was crying. "I've just—I've always been like that. When I want something, I want it. I don't think about how it affects other people. I'm just—I'm just like my mother, who left. She left without thinking how it would affect us."

"You idiot," Javi said. But this time his voice was gentle.

"It wasn't your fault," Pippa said.

"You were angry," Javi said. "That's only human."

"You can't feel only one emotion," Pippa said. "They're all bound up together. Love's part of anger. And anger's part of love. It's all hopelessly confused. That's why the standard stringbind is wrong. All the emotions should be represented."

Javi pushed *The Book of Muse* toward Legacy. "Now what do you see?" he said.

Legacy looked. She shook her head. The letters were becoming clearer, but she still couldn't read them.

"Maybe it takes time," Pippa said.

"Let's sleep on it," Javi said. "You need your rest. You have a big match to play in the morning."

When Pippa came back to Legacy's room in the morning, they checked the book one more time. It still wasn't clear enough to read.

"Are you sure you want to play with that racket?" Pippa said. She looked tired, as if she hadn't slept in days. She'd bitten her fingernails down to the quick.

Legacy tried to smile in a way that would look reassuring. "I'm not giving up now," she said.

"It's too dangerous to summon grana," Pippa said.

"I know," Legacy said. "I won't. And if I win, we'll change the strings tonight."

Pippa nodded. Then she pulled out her velvet-lined box. Legacy shook her head. "No," she said. "I want to keep my face bare."

They both examined her in the mirror. She was wearing her burlap shift, and her hair was loose.

"They'll expect the same paint," Pippa said. "And the same clothes."

"Let them," Legacy said. Then she picked up her racket.

The courts were set up in the same way they had been for the qualifiers—the upper rows converted into stands—but this time many more people had come. The spectators stretched up to the highest tiers of courts in the farthest distance, which had been reserved for spectators from the provinces. Those tiers were sparsely populated, but every other row was full of city dwellers in their silks. They held signs, shouted names, hoisted their children up on their shoulders.

But as Legacy walked on court, the crowd hushed. There was a new, uncomfortable silence. Paula's voice through the speakers broke the silence.

"Well, this is an odd choice, I must say," she said.

Angelo was silent. He watched Legacy take her place on the baseline, then he took a sip from his flask.

"A provi burlap shift," Paula was saying. "Instead of her academy clothes. What can Legacy Petrin be saying?"

She went on, but Legacy didn't let herself listen. She couldn't afford to feel any anger. She couldn't afford to feel anything at all, not with her malfunctioning racket.

Instead, Legacy narrowed her eyes. She peered at her opponent. It was the first time she had played one of the elites. Legacy remembered seeing them on those secret courts. She remembered the snowdrifts that had piled up around Sondra. She wondered which secret botanical amplifiers lurked in the red wax on her opponent's strings.

Pietro Casta was one of Sondra's crew: an older boy whose skin was so pale you could see the blue veins in his arms. When he looked at her before he served, the color seemed to be drained from his eyes. The only pigment on his face was the jagged blue line of paint that split his forehead into hemispheres.

As soon as he served, Legacy felt the temperature on her side of the court shift. By the third game, Pietro was pinning her to the baseline with powerful ground strokes, and the clouds on her side of the court had turned purple as a bruise. By the fourth game they'd lowered, so that Legacy felt as if she could almost swipe them with her racket. It had gotten colder as well: even the city dwellers on her side of the court began to put on extra layers, and some of their children were crying.

"These clouds are getting ominous," Paula said. "And feel that chill in the air! We might have a hailstorm coming."

Legacy knew she couldn't summon any grana. It would only shoot back up her arm. It could even kill her.

By the end of the fifth game, freezing rain had started to fall in icy cold needles. The water on the court began to freeze into slippery puddles. She barely won that game, and by the time the next one started, the icy needles had turned into hailstones the size of frozen golf balls, and Legacy was so busy dodging them and slipping on the frozen puddles that she lost her serve.

By the time she'd lost the first set, she was desperate. Switching sides, and taking refuge from the hailstones under the referee's chair, she closed her eyes. She thought of the elites, training on those secret courts, amplifying with botanical tinctures. She thought of her own stringbind, which was keeping her from expressing anything outward.

A self disguised is a death surmised, she said to herself.

Then her fingertips started to warm. A familiar tingle ran along the roots of her hair.

Her eyes flew open in fright. Knowing that she had to do something to keep herself from expressing grana, she knelt and touched her fingertips to one of the patches of ice that had formed on her side of the net.

Immediately it melted. Her fingers cooled. Legacy smiled to herself. When she glanced up at the crowd, she saw Pippa and Javi in the academy section, jumping up and down and cheering for her. Her smile widened. She knew how to deal with this problem.

As she moved across the court, Legacy allowed herself to summon just enough grana that her fingers warmed. She knelt again and pressed her palm to a patch of ice on the ground. The warmth spread from her hand in a circle, forming a puddle of water that steamed and evaporated within a few seconds.

By the time she'd reached the baseline, she'd unfrozen her court. Pietro was glaring at her. The sleet was still falling in needles, but she felt it melt as soon as it touched her warm shoulders.

Now she bounced the ball once. She bounced the ball twice. Then she closed her eyes and remembered training at night, harnessed to the enormous silk kite. She remembered the wind in her unbraided hair. She remembered the feeling of flying.

When she opened her eyes, everything but the ball and the court disappeared, and she served as though she were alone, running around on the court, with only Javi watching her on the sideline.

There were a few slippery spots still on the court and puddles to navigate when she sprinted toward drop shots, but Legacy glided through them as though there were wheels on her sneakers. When she won that game, she glanced up and saw Javi jumping up and down in the stands, looking even more enthusiastic than Pippa.

By the time she'd won the second set, Pietro was tired. Between sets, he put on a recovery sleeve. And when he returned to begin the last set, his grana was less focused, and the sleet had turned into a drizzle. Then Legacy turned off her grana and turned on her power instead. Soon she'd pinned Pietro to the baseline. She was attacking even his strongest shots, leaping forward to volley as though a trampoline were underfoot.

Overhead, if Paula was talking, Legacy didn't hear her. If the crowd was cheering for Pietro, Legacy didn't hear them, either. She was just playing. She was playing as she always had: wearing her burlap shift, counting her footsteps, listening for the *ping* of the ball striking her strings.

When she won the match, she waved up at the crowds, then ran into the palace to meet with Pippa and Javi.

———————————

"He got tired," Javi said when Legacy got back to her room.

"His elbow injury," Pippa said.

"That's what did him in," Javi said. "Not your grana."

"That level of grana," Pippa said, "is not gonna cut it tomorrow. Not when you're playing Villy."

Legacy took *The Book of Muse* out of her drawer. She flipped through the pages.

"And it certainly won't cut it against Gia," Javi said.

"She's fresh," Pippa said. "And she's been gunning for you since the trials, and—"

"It's here!" Legacy said. "I can read it!"

There, on the seventh page, was the recipe for a stringbind for players of the light grana.

Pippa leaned over Legacy's shoulder.

The letters in the recipe were still a little faint, but Legacy was almost sure she could read them.

"Two threads of metium," Pippa said, peering closer to the page. "Six threads of cormorant feather—that's a natural binder—nine threads of owl claw—that's a trace source of the other minerals—and a weft of corasite threads."

Then she raced out, followed by Legacy and Javi. As they ran through the palace walls, they could catch the sounds of cheering through the open windows. Outside, Silla, Lucco, Argenti, and Polroy would be standing on their raised platform, surrounded by glass, receiving the salutes of the other winners. As they climbed the stairs to the forbidden top floor, they didn't have to worry about anyone finding them in the workshop: everyone was outside watching the matches.

Even the cats seemed to have abandoned the workshop, so Pippa and Javi and Legacy were alone as they rooted around among the glass vials of botanical tinctures, the pots of wax, the metal powders, and the richly hued bolts of fabric.

After a while, Pippa checked the collection of threads that she'd gathered. "I've got everything," she said, "except corasite threads. I can't find any in the whole workshop."

"What do you mean?" Javi said. "Try another box. They must be in here."

But no matter how many boxes Pippa tried, there weren't any threads of corasite.

"Is there powder of corasite?" Legacy asked. "Could we make a thread?"

"That's gone too," Pippa said, holding up an empty porcelain pot.

"Okay," Legacy said. "Then we'll have to find corasite somewhere else. Don't they mine it? Couldn't we buy some?"

Pippa pulled out her copy of *Capulan's Encyclopedia.*

"It's not mined," she said after perusing the pages for a while. "Compound of corasite is obtained by crushing the seedpod of a drammus."

"Oh boy," Javi said. He put his head in his hands.

"I don't understand," Legacy said. "Aren't the minerals mined?"

Pippa sighed. "Most of them are. They're generally most concentrated in metals and stones. But some can only be found in vegetable sources."

"Like this one," Legacy said.

Pippa nodded. "Which wouldn't be a problem," she said, "except that the drammus has been extinct since the Great Fire."

"Wait," Legacy said. "There's one more. I've seen it in the Forest of Cora."

"But that's miles away," Javi said. "Even if we could find out how to get our hands on a cart, it would take days to get there and back."

Legacy felt her stomach sink. After all their work—after taming a pyrus, surviving the cafeteria, learning how to summon her grana, and surviving a near-fatal brush with a stringbind—she couldn't believe her chances at winning the tournament were about to be crushed by the lack of a stupid mineral.

She let her forehead fall into her palms. They were cold and hard as the ground when she'd knelt before Gus. Then Legacy looked at Pippa and Javi.

163

"Gus!" she said. And then they were rushing for the exit, Legacy first, and everything seemed to be falling into place until Legacy swung open the door and saw a pair of gleaming black shoes.

When she looked up, she saw a silvery scarf.

Lucco stared down at her. "Where," he said, "are you children off to?"

CHAPTER SIXTEEN

THE LAST
DRAMMUS

1ucco locked the door behind him. When he turned to face Legacy, Pippa, and Javi, they'd backed into a corner that was clustered with enormous bolts of old fabric.

"How dare you sneak in here?" he said. He was focusing on Pippa, glaring at her with eyes that looked as if they could cut through waxed strings. "How dare you disobey me? When Silla told me to plant that fatal stringbind, I thought it would be fine. I thought my own daughter wouldn't steal from me. Up until I watched that match against Robby Groggio, when her grana redirected because of the stringbind I'd planted, I trusted you to obey me and never come up here. How wrong I was! Do you have any idea what you've done? You could have killed her. You could have ended up in Epinmo, not to mention the embarrassment you'd bring to our family!"

Pippa tried to speak, choked on her words, and started crying.

"You never should have come to the palace," Lucco said. "You weren't cut out for this. You weren't meant to be a stringer. It took you years to match, longer than anyone else. And why was that, do you think? Why do you think you never matched with a player?"

Legacy looked at Pippa. She was trying to speak, but her shoulders were shaking from crying so hard. Lucco was still railing on, but Legacy couldn't sit back and listen any longer. Finally, she stepped forward, away from the fabric.

"She came to the palace," Legacy said, "because she was meant to be a stringer."

Startled by the interruption, Lucco fell silent. Legacy took another step forward.

"In the very beginning," Legacy said, "before I even felt it, she knew there was something wrong with my stringbind. You think you're so smart with your metium-based 'standard bind,' but you didn't fool her for a moment. She could hear it. She could *feel* it. She knew it was keeping me from expressing, even when I didn't believe her."

Lucco remained quiet, but he was looking at Pippa with his head cocked to one side, as though for a moment he wasn't quite sure who she was.

"She has a gift," Legacy said. "Not to mention how hard she works. Not to mention how much courage she's shown! She's ridden with me on a pyrus. She's escaped from your thread cats. She's broken your rules and snuck into forbidden places, all to help me become the player I was meant to become. How can you tell her now she wasn't meant to be a stringer? How can you tell her to be someone she isn't?"

Then, suddenly, Legacy remembered that she was talking to an adult. She was lecturing him as if he were one of the littles. She took a step back and looked down at the floor.

The silence seemed to stretch on forever. Finally, Lucco unlocked the door. When he turned, he focused on Pippa. "Go," he said. "Look out for the cats. And know that you're on your own now. If you get caught, I'll deny that I helped you. I have other children to look out for. I can't risk a term in Epinmo to assist you."

Pippa nodded. She wiped the last tear from her cheek. Her face was still pale, but she stood very straight, then turned and led her friends through the open door of the workshop.

———

By the time Legacy, Pippa, and Javi snuck out of the palace and ran toward the stable, the crowds had gone home. The sun had set, leaving only a smudge of orange on the horizon and a faint golden glow on the domes of the buildings. The upper courts that had been turned into stands were littered with trash: orange peels and whistles and knockoff tapestries supporting various players. The platforms were empty. The main court seemed oddly lonely without any players running across it.

Inside the barn, the lurals growled. The pyruses breathed smoke. They seemed more restless and unhappy than they usually did, maybe because they'd been pent up since the nationals started. But when Legacy came to Gus's stall, he moved toward her with his ears pointing up. His brown eyes were big and gentle.

She scratched his velvety chin and kissed his nose, then led him out of the stable. Outside, Pippa climbed on behind her. Javi hung back, shaking his head.

"We need you," Legacy said.

"Please," Pippa said.

Javi shook his head. "You owe me," he said, glaring at Legacy. Then he squeezed his eyes shut and climbed on, all three of them crowding close to fit between Gus's wings.

"To the provinces, Gus," Legacy whispered in his ear. Then he was surging up into the air, his magnificent wings flapping beneath them.

Legacy smiled. Javi had been gripping her shirt so hard it strained at her neck, but as they leveled off she noticed that his grip loosened, and when she looked behind her, he was gazing wide-eyed at the world below. The city was growing small underneath them. Now it was no more than a sprawl of twinkling lights, the river shining dark near the wall, and the cycapress trees twisting darker than darkness. Legacy directed Gus with her knees, and they moved out into the provinces, over Minori and Agricio, and approached the Forest of Cora.

Even from high above, Legacy could smell the familiar scents of her home: even in the darkness, she could smell the dusty green of the olive trees, the fresh soil wafting up from the fields, and finally the charcoal scent of the forest. For a while, they circled over the vast expanse of burnt drammus trees, until—peering into the darkness for that single cleared rectangle in the forest—Legacy finally found what they'd come for.

She urged Gus down. He angled himself toward the earth until his hooves struck the soft, overgrown grass of the tennis court in the Forest of Cora.

"What *is* this place?" Pippa said, her green eyes wide and her mouth slightly agape.

"I have no idea," Legacy said.

"Neither do I," Javi said. "But that, right there, is a drammus."

It was even more beautiful than Legacy remembered. The delicate leaves shivered slightly in the night breeze. Their green scent reminded Legacy of the way the branches had stroked her cheek the day before she snuck into the city. She remembered how, with her eyes closed, it had almost seemed as if her mother were whispering encouragement.

Now she wished she could sit down under those branches again. She wished she could stay here forever, or at least run home to the orphanage, snuggle in beside Ink, give Van a hug, tell her father how much she loved him. Remembering what her life used to be like, she stood still as stone under the drammus, incapable of moving in any direction. It was Pippa who plucked the desiccated seedpod. Javi stashed it in his pocket.

"Come on, Leg," Pippa said, tugging her arm. "It's creepy out here in the darkness."

"We have to hurry," Javi said. "There's barely enough time to get back before your next match."

Still, Legacy remained rooted in place. She glanced over her shoulder at Gus. He was watching her with his big brown eyes as if he knew how much she wanted to stay. As if he almost wanted to let her.

But then he bent onto his forelegs and lowered his head. Legacy smiled. It was time to go. She had to finish what she'd started.

Once she'd climbed on, Pippa and Javi joined her. She held on to Gus's thick mane and whispered into the caverns of his ears, and soon they were winging over the forest, past Agricio, flying fast toward the towers and domes of the city.

Back in Legacy's room, Pippa took a tiny silver hammer out of her box. Using a little porcelain pestle, she began to grind the seedpod in a porcelain pot the size of a thimble. Legacy watched over her shoulder while the ground bits slowly changed color, giving way to a fine vermilion mineral powder.

"Now I have to mix the powder with water," Pippa said, "and heat until it thickens into a paste. Then I can draw it through this." She held up what looked like a silver ruler, studded with little holes of different sizes. "Once the paste is drawn through the holes, it comes out like long strands of spaghetti. I'll weave them into the racket as soon as they're cool enough to touch."

Outside Legacy's window, the sun had risen. The grass courts were rosy pink, and people had begun to filter in from the city, carrying their banners and whistles, their children hoisted up on their shoulders.

By the time Pippa had heated the corasite, the stands were already packed.

Javi stood by the window. "It's almost time," he said. "You'll have to play Villy with the old strings."

Legacy nodded. She joined him by the window. She watched the crowd taking its places and noted that, in the highest courts, there were far more people from the provinces than there had been yesterday.

"They've come to support you," Javi said.

"The burlap shift," Legacy said.

"You're one of them," Javi said.

Legacy looked at him. "We're two of them," she said.

Javi looked down. "Sort of," he said. "Though it's not easy fitting in anywhere—city or provinces—with one of these on your neck."

Legacy reached forward and touched it gently. "When did it happen?" she said.

Javi shrugged. "I was pretty little. My mom had supported our family by making dyes for the silks, but her eyesight started fading. She couldn't see after a while. Something about the minerals in the dyes. My father tended a wealthy merchant's garden, but it wasn't enough to keep food on the table. One day he took a chicken. They caught him on the way out. After the trial, they branded my parents, and me and my sister. I don't remember it hurting too much. I think I might have blacked out. I just remember waiting for the brand to land on my neck and the smell of skin burning."

Legacy thought of Javi as a little boy, waiting for the brand to burn the skin on his neck, and she felt something sharp and hard scraping the inside of her stomach. She felt her skin growing warm. Suddenly Pippa stepped forward in alarm.

"Stop!" she said, shaking Legacy by the shoulder.

Legacy smiled. Her skin cooled. "I know, I know." Then she looked at Javi. "Scar or no," she said, "you're one of us now."

He smiled, and Pippa bit her thumbnail and nervously hovered. "You have to be careful not to summon too much," Pippa said. "It could be dangerous to—"

"*I know*," Legacy said.

Pippa smiled bashfully. "I know you do."

Before heading out, Legacy looked at herself in the mirror one more time. There she was: a girl from the provinces. Going out to play the semifinals of the nationals. Against the second-ranked kid in the republic.

———————

Villy's shots were powerful, but they weren't stronger than Gus's fireballs. And they certainly weren't scarier. So Legacy didn't flinch when his shots were rocketing toward her. She absorbed their power. Then she made them her own.

Even when the clouds lowered over her head and snow started eddying down, Legacy didn't stop attacking his shots. Her aggression must have startled him, or interrupted his concentration, because he wasn't ever able to summon the blizzard she'd seen through the window on the practice courts.

Between serves, he whipped his calf with his racket. He seemed to be yelling at himself when he walked to the other side of the service line.

"It looks like our provincial champion's keeping her cool better than Villy," Angelo said into the loudspeaker.

"For now," Paula said. She said something else, but Legacy didn't hear her. She couldn't afford to get angry, not with her malfunctioning strings. She couldn't afford to get heated.

She tried to stay just warm enough to melt the occasional drifts of snow that began to pile up. Otherwise, she played as she'd played every morning in practice. She tried not to look up at Silla. She tried not to glance out at the crowd.

Villy, however, kept looking out. He stared up at the most distant courts, which were now full of provis. They were shouting, calling Legacy's name, and their cheers seemed to anger him. He lost focus. By the third set, he wasn't even summoning any snow, and Legacy pulled ahead.

Only when she'd hit the final shot, winning the match, did she allow herself to look at the crowd. Then she saw that the city dwellers were seated, staring at her in shock. And beyond them, in the distance, the provis were standing. They were stamping their feet. They were beating the sky with their fists. Legacy heard her name surging out from the stands. The sound rolled over her, louder and louder, a chant they were all singing.

Legacy smiled. She thought of where they'd come from: those shanties in Mino. Her heart seemed to grow larger in her chest, and then once again she felt that familiar warming in her fingertips and tingling in the roots of her hair.

It was all one: her love for them and her anger at how they lived. It was that claw in her stomach, which was now growing warmer and larger until it came full circle. Then it was a gold orb that lit her up from within.

She waved toward the upper tiers of the crowd. She lifted her hands over her head. She grinned and pumped her fists in triumph, and her fans cheered and clapped and called her name. Legacy was so absorbed in the moment that she only just remembered to salute Silla before heading back toward the palace.

In Legacy's bedroom—the windows closed and the cracks in the door sealed to keep out the cats—Pippa had pulled the corasite strings. Now she sat with Legacy's racket on her lap and the strings spooled on various spindles.

"Okay," Pippa said, "now tell me a story."

Legacy sat beside her on the bed and told her about that morning when she'd approached the provincial trials. How overwhelmed she'd been when she walked into the tent that looked like an enormous meringue. How she'd listened to that woman with the gem-encrusted glasses, and how she'd played her way up from the bottom court to the top court by imagining she was playing against the orphanage wall.

And she told Pippa about how, in her final match, she'd felt such sympathy for Jenni Bruno, with her broad shoulders, her cropped silver hair, and the silver dust caking her nails. How she'd loved Jenni Bruno, and how she'd beaten her anyway. And how, at the end, Jenni Bruno had clasped her hand and told her to win the nationals. To win them for the provinces.

While Legacy talked, Pippa wove. And when she'd finished the story, Legacy looked down at the strings. Pippa had woven a glistening tapestry into the head of the racket, a complicated weave of mineral threads, patterns of dark color swirling on a background of vermilion.

"I think I got it," Pippa said.

"You're sure?" Javi said. He was pacing under the portrait of Silla.

"No," Pippa said. "But that's the best I can do."

Javi stopped pacing. He looked at Legacy. "You're sure the two of you read the ingredients right?" he said.

"I think so," Legacy said.

Pippa plucked the strings a few times, holding the racket close to her ear. "It sounds right to me," she said. "I think it's on key."

Then Legacy picked up the racket. She looked at herself in the mirror. She tried not to think about how spidery the lettering in the book was when she and Pippa read the ingredients. She tried not to think about that flash of pain in her arm when she'd summoned her grana with the wrong strings. She tried not to think about Gia training all those nights on the secret courts. She tried not to think about Gia waxing her strings with amplifying botanicals.

She refused to think about any of that. She just looked herself in the mirror again and held on to her racket.

Legacy Petrin, she thought. *It's time to win the nationals.*

CHAPTER SEVENTEEN

THE HOWL OF
A LURAL

In the doorway out to the courts, Legacy paused for a moment. She could hear the sounds of the crowd, and the voices of Paula and Angelo, filtering into the palace.

"The upper stands are full today," Angelo was saying. "It appears that our provis have turned out in unprecedented numbers."

His voice sounded clearer than usual. As Legacy moved toward the announcers' stand, getting ready to take her place on court, she noticed that his silks were neater too. It seemed as if he'd combed his hair. And it almost seemed as if he'd abstained from whatever it was he kept in his flask.

"There does," Paula said, her voice somewhat icy, "appear to be a preponderance of burlap in the upper stands."

"And not only the upper stands, Paula," Angelo said. "From where I'm sitting, I see quite a few city kids wearing burlap like Legacy Petrin's."

"A newcomer's always interesting," Paula said, in the same prickly tone. "But of course, from where I'm sitting, there are just as many people wearing Gia's signature braid. People might like an underdog, but they're also drawn to excellence."

Legacy moved out into the sunshine and lifted one hand. As soon

175

as she did, as if on cue, the upper rows of the stadium rose. Legacy felt her heartbeat getting stronger, but there was also a pounding coming from somewhere else, somewhere outside of her body.

In unison, in the upper rows, the spectators were all stomping their feet. It sounded like a march. It sounded like her own heartbeat.

Legacy smiled. They roared louder in response. She moved out on the court to face Gia.

With her single braid, wearing a short black dress with pleated skirt and long sleeves, Gia looked sleek and powerful. From the first point, she played with a ferocity that set Legacy on the defensive.

The first game was quick. Gia served, and followed her serves up to net, aggressively volleying Legacy's returns. When she won, she roared in triumph. She pumped her fist up to the sky. The lower stands of the audience roared in unison with her.

Legacy served the second game. Her heart had migrated up from her chest and lodged itself uncomfortably over her sternum. She hadn't expected Gia to come on so strong. Hoping to settle her mind, Legacy bounced the ball a few times before she threw the first toss. But when she'd palmed the ball again, she glanced up at the sky. The clouds over her side of the court had grown dark.

It was still technically morning, and only a few moments ago it had been sunny. But now there was a new chill in the air, as if evening were approaching.

Legacy swallowed. She tossed the ball high and hit a good serve. But it wasn't good enough. Gia pounced on it early, attacking the ball with so much spin that her return skidded past Legacy's backhand.

Nervously, while she walked to the other side of the court, Legacy looked up at the sky. It was getting darker. And she wasn't glowing.

Her fingers weren't even warm. She couldn't manage to feel anything other than nervous.

The next game, Gia renewed her aggression. Meanwhile, the light continued to drain out of the sky on Legacy's side of the court. The darkness reached its fingers up into the tiers of audience seats. Now hawkers in her side of the stands had begun to move up and down in the aisles, selling jackets and headlamps. Every time Gia won a point and pumped her fist in triumph, the air around Legacy grew a little more impenetrable.

When Gia won her third serve, she screamed up toward the top rows of the stadium. Legacy watched bats begin to stream out of the ramparts of the palace. They thronged in the air overheard, a tumult that only unnerved Legacy further.

By the time Gia was up 5–3 in the first set, Legacy still wasn't glowing. It was becoming difficult to see the ball in the darkness. She tried to move according to sound, listening for her own footsteps, focusing on the *ping* of the ball on Gia's strings, but she often got a late start. Then, by the time she'd seen the form of the ball shooting toward her, it was already too late. She couldn't pounce. She couldn't throw her weight into the ball. Sometimes she missed the shot completely or took it on the frame of the racket, sending it ricocheting into the crowds.

Between points, desperate thoughts began to run through Legacy's mind. What if, after all the work she and Javi and Pippa had done, she couldn't summon her grana with this new racket? What if she'd misread the recipe? What if Pippa hadn't woven her story right?

Then she'd never be able to summon her grana. The darkness

177

would only get more and more impenetrable, and Legacy would lose the match.

She wouldn't win enough money to keep the orphanage open. Silla would have succeeded in manipulating her through her strings. And Legacy would have to slink back to her father, defeated.

By the last game of the set, Legacy was so anxious that she double-faulted two serves. Gia won the game and the set. The crowds in the lower parts of the stadium took to their feet and started chanting, "Gia," together, their voices rising like a wave and falling over Legacy as she sat down on her bench.

"It looks like our provi won't pull this one off," Paula said with an unmistakable note of triumph in her voice.

On her bench, between sets, Legacy sat in the darkness that was so thick she felt as though she'd fallen into it and would never manage to crawl out again. The outlines of things—the referee stand, the net, even the massive palace behind her—had begun to lose their sharp edges, as though everything besides Legacy were disappearing.

The cool evening air was stiffening her muscles. And she couldn't think straight. All she could concentrate on was the fact that she was disappointing everyone.

Overhead, Paula was talking about Gia's "natural class." She was going on in a smug tone of voice about Gia's superior tactics and the accuracy of her serve, and meanwhile Legacy racked her brain for how she could summon her light.

She tried to get angry. When that didn't work, she remembered that her anger was connected to her love, so she tried to think about her father. About Pippa and Javi, about flying on Gus's back.

Still, her fingers were cold. The roots of her hair weren't tingling.

Legacy glanced up at the crowds. Most of them were cheering for Gia. But off in the distance, the highest rows were packed with provis, and some of them were standing and waving, holding signs with her name. They were all wearing burlap. Their hair was loose and unbraided.

Their support warmed her a little. It almost felt as if they were reaching down from the stands to embrace her. Then Legacy thought of Jenni Bruno. She thought of all the other provis who might be trapped underground or spending their days in factories. Kids who couldn't come to the stadium today but whom she was here to represent. She remembered the shantytown and the flames billowing above the massive factories.

Feeling stronger and more determined, she picked up her racket. She walked on court. And though she was moving through the darkness, she realized that there was a little flickering cone of light cast before her, as though she were wearing a headlamp. And this time, when Gia served, she could see the ball as it approached.

Now she was able to get to the ball earlier. Her racket started to sing a little more clearly. Legacy felt stronger, and more certain. Her side of the court was still dark, but she'd played in the darkness before. She'd played outside the orphanage when it still wasn't light. She'd played at the academy when the sun hadn't come up.

She won her serve. She broke Gia's serve after that. Gia seemed to be getting nervous. She kept touching her braid and muttering to herself under her breath. Every time Gia showed how nervous she was, Legacy felt calmer. Now she felt the soft grass underfoot. She counted her footsteps. She played well enough that she took Gia to a tiebreaker

179

in the second set. When she managed to win, breaking Gia's serve, Gia threw her racket at the back wall and released a cry of frustration.

It was a terrifying sound, like the howl of a lural. It made the hairs on Legacy's arm stand up. She remembered Pippa telling her that Gia had been brought to the academy when she was an infant. Gia's parents had died. She'd been raised by Silla to become a champion.

This was all she had, Legacy realized. Winning was who she was. Now Legacy was threatening that.

No wonder Gia had howled like that, Legacy thought. No wonder her mind was full of darkness.

When Legacy took her bench between sets, she tried to eat a packet of her recovery goo, but she couldn't swallow it. Energy in the stadium was shifting. It had been shifting since Gia threw her racket and howled. Legacy could feel Gia's rage as a mounting pressure in the air, like the tension in the atmosphere a few minutes before a thunderstorm hits.

When she glanced at Gia on her bench, she saw that Gia was staring at her. Over the black lines of her paint, Gia's eyes were so black they were like holes punched out of the pale paper mask of her face.

———

When Legacy walked toward the service box for the first point of the third set, she felt a spatter of rain on her arm. She looked up. Earlier, when she started pinning Gia to the baseline, the sky had grown lighter. The darkness had broken up, allowing rays of light to shine through.

But now the clouds had gathered again. They loomed thick and low, the blackish purple color of plums.

When Gia served, the rain kicked up harder. By the end of that game, it was coming down in sheets that caused the ball to skid off in unpredictable directions. And though Legacy was still glowing, her light was flickering fainter than it had in the second set. She moved around her side of the court like a lantern in a rainstorm.

By the time Gia was up 3–1 in the third set, the rain was coming down even harder. The court was getting muddier. Huge booms of thunder caused Legacy's heart to skid in her chest, and occasional jags of lightning seemed to tear the stadium open.

A few times, Legacy almost slipped. In the fifth game of the set, she lunged toward a drop shot, then skidded forward in a thick slick of mud. When she tried to pull short, she fell sideways, landing hard on her hip.

Gia pumped her fist. She roared up at the sky. Facedown in the mud, Legacy felt anger beginning to build in her chest.

"That was an embarrassing spill!" Paula was saying. "Mortifying! Humiliating, for Legacy Petrin!"

Humiliating? Legacy thought. Embarrassing? What about painful? What about dangerous?

When Legacy stood up again, her shift was soaking wet. It clung to her arms and her legs. She was cold and her hip hurt, and the crowd was pointing, clutching their stomachs, and laughing at how badly she'd fallen.

The claw began to form in Legacy's stomach again. But this time it wasn't the round glowing orb that it had become when she was practicing her grana with Pippa and Javi. It was only the claw: desperate, angry, and incomplete.

As she bent her knees and began swaying in preparation to receive the next serve, straining to see in the darkness, getting pelted by sheets of rain, she was so angry that her racket began to burn in her hands.

It was difficult to hold on to her racket. Realizing that, Legacy tried to push her anger deep into her stomach, but it kept blossoming up again. It was like a snake climbing up her throat and trying to get out of her mouth. She kept trying to swallow it, but her throat started to ache, and she missed the first two of Gia's serves because she was so distracted.

Before the next serve, Legacy moved back to the wall. She touched her fingertips to the stone. Then she blew on them to get them to cool. *Stop*, she said to herself. *You can't feel all this anger.*

But then Legacy remembered what Javi had said: *That's only human.*

Pippa had said it as well. *All the emotions should be represented.*

The snake of Legacy's anger stirred again as she thought of Javi waiting for his neck to be burned. She thought of Javi's family, banished to the provinces. She thought of Pippa's father saying that he couldn't help them; she thought of the refugee camps she'd passed in Mino; she thought of the silver dust under Jenni Bruno's fingernails; she thought of Ink, abandoned on the steps of the orphanage; and when she thought about Van, working in the factories, the snake had pushed up her throat and out of her mouth in the form of a shout.

As she walked back to the baseline, her racket was shining so bright that each stroke cast a wide arc of yellow light through the impenetrable gloom of Gia's rainstorm.

And with each new shot, the arc widened. By the end of the game, Legacy had pushed the darkness and the rain away from her so that it clustered on Gia's side of the court.

Now it was Legacy who was pumping her fist. Now it was Legacy who was screaming to herself in the darkness. She could see the ball again, and her timing had improved. Her service returns had gotten sharper.

On her side of the court, Gia seemed to be growing a little less sure of herself. The thunder had died down, and the stadium was no longer torn open by jags of lightning. It even seemed as if the rain was slowing.

Legacy had just pulled up 4–3 when she heard a strange shift in Paula's voice. "This is strong play from Legacy Petrin," Paula said. "Extraordinarily strong, as you yourself have been saying, Angelo."

For a moment, Legacy was startled. She almost looked up at Paula. But then she reminded herself: *It doesn't matter. It doesn't matter what she thinks of you. You know who you are.*

Legacy adjusted her strings with her fingers. These were her strings, woven with corasite taken from the forest behind the orphanage where she grew up. These were her strings. This was her racket. And this was her tournament, to win as she'd intended.

She bounced the ball once. She bounced the ball twice.

The sky was perfectly clear now. The whole world was glistening, as it did when the sun came out after a rain.

Finally, Legacy tossed the ball overhead, reared back, and unfurled her racket over her shoulder. The serve sang so true on her strings that even she knew Gia wouldn't be able to reach it.

After that, she won point after point. Overhead, on the platform, Angelo was laughing. "Have you ever seen such a racket?" he was saying. "Look at it shining!"

But what he said didn't matter, just as Paula's response didn't matter. Now the provis were back up on their feet, and soon the city dwellers were standing too. They'd started stomping in unison with the provis.

Even that didn't matter. All that mattered was the *ping* of the ball

183

striking the racket. How true it was. How it resonated with everything Legacy had always carried within her.

The whole stadium was full of the sound of stomping, one united heartbeat that Legacy felt in her own chest while she ran up to volley.

Somewhere in the distance, she heard Angelo saying: "Look, everyone, look up at the tapestry!"

When Legacy glanced up, she could see it shimmering in the new, splendid light. It was changing color. The figures of Silla and the other senators were growing blurry and strange. As if their outlines were less certain. As if someday, other forms might replace them.

The crowd was still standing—calling Legacy's name, stomping their feet—when Legacy won the last, long point on a deep cross-court that spun beyond Gia's reach, and Gia fell to the ground, and Silla began to descend from her box.

She moved with such grace—her chin up, her shoulders thrown back—that as she approached Legacy at center court, the stomping quieted some. The cheering hushed.

Silla waited for Gia to lift herself from the ground and shake Legacy's hand at the net. For a moment, Legacy was startled: Gia seemed to be ashamed and couldn't lift her eyes to meet Legacy's face. But then Gia fled off court, and Silla lifted the hem of her silks to step across the grass.

When she reached Legacy's side, she lifted Legacy's hand over her head. The crowd stood and roared, and both Silla and Legacy waved.

Silla was smiling. And the crowd's cheering was loud, so it was only Legacy who heard the chilling tone in Silla's voice when she whispered, "You clever girl."

Legacy smiled wider. So did Silla. She lifted Legacy's hand higher over her head.

Now Paula had quieted the crowd. She was speaking into her loudspeaker.

"To whom do you pledge your loyalty?" she shouted.

Legacy smiled at Silla. Silla smiled back. Then Legacy turned out to the crowds.

"I pledge my loyalty to the provinces!" she said.

For a moment, the crowds went perfectly silent.

Then, from the most distant tiers of the crowd, a few claps could be heard. Then, one by one, the provis started stomping. Soon the sound had become overwhelming.

"To the provinces!" Angelo said into his loudspeaker.

Silla's grip on Legacy's wrist became icy. Her fingers were as vicious as talons.

Still, she managed to smile the whole time she presented Legacy with her check. Legacy looked down at the piece of paper. It was enough money to keep the orphanage open. Enough money to send Van to the School of Economics. Enough money to keep a roof over the littles' heads until they were adults.

Legacy took it. Silla smiled even more broadly.

"Ah," she said, between glittering teeth. "So you are your mother's daughter."

Legacy remained where she was, smiling and waving up at the crowds.

"What a shame it would be," Silla said, "for you to meet the same fate."

The provis were still standing, as were some of the city dwellers, clapping and stomping their feet.

"I'll come after you wherever you go," Silla said.

Legacy glanced up at the tapestry. It was still shimmering, its outlines less clear.

"Come after me," Legacy said, surprising even herself with the bold tone of her voice. "Come after me," she said again. "I dare you."

Then she waved once more to the crowds and headed back into the palace.

CHAPTER EIGHTEEN

SHINE

Even though she knew that Silla would be busy with members of the press all night and well into the next day, Legacy didn't feel safe enough in her room at the palace to sleep. Neither did Pippa and Javi.

All night, with the windows closed and the crack in the door sealed with wax, she and Javi and Pippa stayed up making plans. At first, Legacy had tried to argue that Javi and Pippa could stay, but it soon became clear that they couldn't. They'd been a part of her open confrontation with Silla. Silla knew they'd helped her re-string her racket. So if Silla was coming for Legacy, she was coming for Javi and Pippa as well.

The next conversation involved where they'd go when they left the academy. Legacy and Pippa had tried to tell Javi that he should go back to Mino and find his family, but he had responded that he didn't know where they lived anymore, and it could take him months to figure out their whereabouts. In the meantime, he said, who else would help Legacy get back to her training?

"Training can wait," Legacy said, and both Pippa and Javi stared at her as if she'd said that lurals could be cuddly.

"Training can't wait," Javi said.

"The only way we're safe in this country is if you're winning," Pippa said.

Javi nodded. "Silla won't dare to hurt us if the people are still behind you. But the only way to keep them behind you is to keep winning."

"You'll have to play the next major," Pippa said.

"The Capari Open," Javi said.

"Me?" Legacy said, staring in disbelief. "Play a major?"

"You idiot," Javi said. "You just won the nationals!"

By the time the stars had come out over the palace, Legacy and Javi and Pippa had decided to head back to the orphanage together before daylight. Once they'd passed safely through Agricio, Legacy and Javi could train on the court in the Forest of Cora, and Pippa could study the Ancient Stringing techniques that Legacy would need to keep winning.

Once they'd decided they would all leave the palace by morning, the hardest part was figuring out what to do about Gus. Legacy thought about taking him with her, but Javi put his foot down.

"You can't give Silla any excuse," he said. "Steal property of the palace, and she'll make it public. She'll make it into an issue. Then, once public opinion has shifted, she'll clap you straight in Epinmo. She'll clap us all straight in Epinmo."

Legacy finally had to give in. Around four in the morning, just before they took off, Legacy and Javi and Pippa snuck out to the stable.

As soon as she walked in, Gus came to the grate and shoved his nose through. He watched her with his big gentle eyes, waiting for her to let him out.

Legacy stood at the door of his stall. She pressed her nose to his nose. She breathed his fur and smelled his familiar horsey scent. She scratched his velvety chin. "Running, leaping, flying, start," she whispered. "Now you'll find your gentle heart."

He seemed to understand, but he didn't back away from the grate. She could feel him watching her as she walked away.

On their way out of the barn, Pippa slung her arm around Legacy's shoulder. Even Javi looked shaken. In fact, Legacy noticed, Javi looked awful. Despite all his big talk about leaving Gus behind, as they walked over the courts toward the palace gates he was ashen and silent. And when he ran back to get the whistle he'd accidentally left, Legacy wondered if he'd gone back because he didn't want them to see him start crying.

Javi was more cheerful when he caught up with them at the gates. And now, as they moved down the same busy, winding streets Legacy had moved up for the first time only a few weeks before, it was Pippa she worried about.

Legacy watched her out of the corner of her eye for signs that she was sad about leaving the city where she'd grown up. The whole way down to the river, Pippa kept her green eyes trained on the shops they passed. She focused hard on the lemon-shaped soaps, the wooden horses, the glass lampshades. When Legacy caught a glimpse of her friend's reflection in the windows, she could tell that Pippa was trying not to let her lower lip tremble.

"You okay, Pippa?" Legacy said.

Pippa turned and forced a bright smile. "Never better," she said.

She pulled her father's copy of *Capulan's Encyclopedia of Minerals and Botanicals* from under her coat. "Now I won't have to hide when I'm studying up on the old ways."

Javi rolled his eyes. "Please," he said, "spare us the Ancient Stringing Craft lectures."

"At least I don't take bribes," Pippa said.

"There won't be any bribes to take in the provinces," Javi said.

They kept bickering in the background while they crossed the Butchers' Bridge and headed out toward the city walls. Everywhere they went, people were staring at Legacy or smiling shyly.

Legacy smiled back. She tried not to look frightened. She tried not to think about Silla speaking to her through that fake smile: *I'll come after you wherever you go.* And, *What a shame it would be for you to meet the same fate.*

When they reached the road that led toward the provinces, the first cart that passed was carrying a load of mining equipment. A few yards after it passed them, it pulled up short.

"Legacy Petrin!" the driver said. He was grinning ear to ear, showing two silver prosite teeth.

For a moment, looking up at the grinning driver, Legacy felt a moment of sorrow. She'd never again be as free as she was when she snuck out of the orphanage and hopped a ride on that chicken cart. Now she was a person people recognized. She was Legacy Petrin. They had an idea of who she was.

Then she remembered the provis cheering. She remembered that this was her destiny. It had been written for her in her mother's own hand, stitched into *The Book of Muse.*

She smiled up at the driver. "Could we get a ride to the Forest of Cora?" Legacy said.

"It would be my honor to take you to Minori," he said. "But that's where I stop."

"It's a start at least," Pippa said, trying to sound cheerful.

Once they'd climbed on board beside the driver, Legacy glanced over her shoulder at the bed of the cart. It was full of mining equipment, not frightened chickens. Legacy forced herself to turn and face forward. The city grew smaller behind them. Then they were approaching the ramshackle huts that sprawled out from the mines, and the driver turned to Legacy.

"Here's where I stop," he said. "You can wait here for another cart and see if that one's heading out to the Forest of Cora."

"Thank you," Legacy said.

He grinned, showing his silver teeth. "Thank *you*," he said. "I've got a little daughter at home. We watched your match together. I've never seen her so happy." Then he flicked his reins and rode off. "Good luck, Legacy Petrin!" he called over his shoulder.

From the side of the road, they watched his cart wind its way toward the terraced sides of the mines, and when it had disappeared behind a layer of oily smoke, Legacy turned toward Javi.

He was staring out at the tents and at the trucks crawling out of the mines.

"You're sure you don't want to stop here?" Legacy said. "We could go on without you."

Javi shook his head. "It's okay. I haven't seen my family for a long time. And we have a tournament to get ready for."

While they waited in silence by the side of the road, Legacy thought about how much her friends had given up for her sake. That thought darkened her mind until she looked up and saw a splotch in the sky, circling toward them.

"Gus!" she said. Her face broke into a grin. Then she glanced at Javi.

He looked down at his feet. "I might have accidentally left the stable door open."

Legacy was laughing out loud when Gus landed beside them. She threw her arms around his neck. He pushed his velvety nose into her cheek.

For a while, Legacy couldn't stop laughing and kissing Gus. Then she remembered all of Javi's warnings.

She looked at Javi. "But what if Silla blames us for this?"

Javi gave her a wry smile and gestured toward the scar on his neck. "I'm only living up to my reputation."

"That's not funny," Legacy said.

"I know," Javi said. "But it's not right, the way they keep those animals in the stable. And anyway, I have faith in you. You keep playing the way you did in the finals, and no one in the republic will buy any stories Silla tells about pyruses, stolen or otherwise."

Once they'd climbed aboard Gus, they flew over the deep rust-red holes in the mountainsides. They flew over Agricio, where Legacy could see the forms of crackles hunched in the olive trees. Then, finally, Legacy saw the burnt Forest of Cora in the distance. Gus circled down toward the orphanage, and his hooves hit the soft earth of the garden.

Legacy and Pippa and Javi hadn't even fully climbed off Gus's back when the littles burst out the kitchen door. Then they all swarmed around Legacy. Leo had jumped into her arms, and Zaza was tugging at her shirt, and all of them were hugging her, and asking her about Gus, and about Gia's rainstorm, and about the food at the palace, and only after obliging them by causing herself to glow on cue did Legacy look up and see Van in the doorway.

"You did it, bud," he said. He was grinning and holding his copy of the *Nova Times* with a picture of Legacy on the front.

"It's true," Legacy said. "I did it."

"I told you you'd win!" Van said. "You didn't believe me."

Legacy hugged him. She felt how frail his shoulders were. As she pulled him closer, she felt his glasses crash into her neck. She thought again how close she'd come to losing him.

"I didn't believe you," she said. "But thank you for believing in me even so."

For a moment, they stood close together and watched the littles. Zaza seemed to have grown a little more bold in Legacy's absence. She'd climbed onto Gus's back and had grabbed a fistful of his mane, and Gus—amazingly—tolerated the assault until Ink stepped forward, unlocked Zaza's fingers, and gently removed her from Gus's back.

Legacy was amazed. Ink seemed to have grown so much in her absence. It seemed like only yesterday when Ink was flouncing around in her cape, bossing around the other littles. Now she was quieter but also somehow more of a presence.

Over Ink's shoulder, Legacy saw her father in the doorway. His arms were crossed over his chest.

Legacy winced. For a moment, she wished she could run away, but then she gathered her courage and urged herself toward him. At the last minute, before following him into the kitchen, Legacy turned and looked back toward her new friends. Pippa smiled at her, gave her

193

the thumbs-up, then busied herself entertaining the littles by showing them the miniature silver corkscrews in her velvet-lined box. Legacy smiled. Even Javi was showing more than his usual patience by allowing Zaza to climb onto his back and examine the fabric of his swishing warm-up suit.

Finally, Legacy turned and followed her father into the kitchen. Before saying anything, she reached into the pocket of her burlap shift and put her money down on the table. "There's enough to take care of the orphanage for a few years," she said. "So Van doesn't have to go to work."

Her father nodded. He still didn't say anything.

Legacy reached into her sack and drew out *The Book of Muse*. She placed it on the table as well. "Why didn't you give me this?" she said.

When she looked up at his face, she expected to see anger. She was surprised, then, to see that he only looked sad. His hair was whiter than she remembered. And when he turned away from her and coughed, his whole body heaved.

Legacy looked down. He'd always had an occasional cough—the result, he said, of breathing too much ash during the fire—but it seemed to have gotten worse since she left for the city. Maybe the stress of running the orphanage without her had run him down.

When he turned back toward Legacy, he sat with her at the table and focused on his hands, which were clasped on the table.

"I wanted to keep you here," he said, "where you'd be safe."

"But you lied to me," Legacy said. "You kept from me what should have been mine."

Her father nodded. He still didn't meet her eyes when he spoke. "Your mother believed that your destiny was to play tennis," he said. "To go back to the city, to become a champion. She believed that. But

I saw what Silla did to her. Banishing her. Keeping her under surveillance. I wanted to spare you the same fate. I thought if I could keep you from playing tennis, I could keep you safe."

"But it's who I *am*," Legacy said. "It's what I was meant to do."

As soon as the words had escaped her, Legacy saw how much they hurt him. For a moment, he closed his eyes, and Legacy almost wished she could pull the words back from the air in between them. It didn't matter. Nothing mattered anymore except how much she loved him.

"I see that now," her father said. "And I'm sorry."

Legacy rushed toward him and draped her arms around his neck. He held her for a while, and when she pulled away from him, she could see that his eyes were watery.

"It's okay, Papa," she said. He smiled, and she knelt at his feet. "But can I ask just one more question?"

Her father nodded.

"Why didn't you tell me who my mother was?" Legacy said.

Her father stroked her hair with one hand. "I suppose I was angry," he said. He thought for a moment, and then he continued. "I came here with her, you know. After Silla banished her. She wanted to start an academy. She wanted it to be a haven for the abandoned children of the provinces. And I wanted whatever she wanted. So we built a court in the forest. We fixed up the orphanage. And we had so much fun while we did it. We laughed together all day. We were brimming over with plans."

For a moment, her father paused. Legacy closed her eyes and tried to imagine her mother laughing. Fixing up the orphanage alongside her father.

"Then you were born, and we were even happier. But something always hovered in the background for her. There was something about a prophecy. Something about a tapestry. I told her to forget it."

"The prognosticating tapestry," Legacy said.

Her father nodded. "Yes. I told her we could prevent any stupid prophecy made out of threads. She disagreed. We argued about it bitterly. Then one morning she left, and I was so angry. Angry because I loved her so much. And angry because I loved you so much, and I couldn't understand how she'd left you. When you grew older, and wanted to know more about her, I didn't want to speak about her to you in anger. So I tried not to. I tried to forget her. I tried to pretend I could forget her."

Legacy sighed. She touched the green cover of the book. "A self disguised is a death surmised," she said.

Her father laughed softly. "You're wiser than I am, sometimes," he said. "But you're still my daughter. And if you disobey me again—"

He didn't finish. He was interrupted by Zaza storming the kitchen, Ink's old cape flying behind her.

"You're needed onstage!" she announced.

When Legacy joined the littles out in the garden, Ink had stationed them in their positions. Leo and Hugo stood at the back, playing excited fans from the provinces. Someone had taped a sign reading "Polroy" to the front of Javi's warm-up suit: his arms were crossed, and he was glaring at Legacy, obviously close to the limits of his tolerance. Pippa, on the other hand, seemed to be having a grand time, twirling a wooden racket, wearing a braided length of blond rope attached to a headband, and showing off her two stripes of black face paint.

Ink, standing center stage, picked up a book. It was a new book, one Legacy hadn't seen. Peering over her shoulder, Legacy realized that the pages were scrawled with Ink's spindly writing.

Smiling, Legacy tousled Ink's curls. How many nights, off in her luxurious room at the academy, had she worried about how the littles would fall asleep without her there to tell stories?

But Ink had learned to create her own stories. She didn't need the old tales anymore. She was ready to start telling new ones.

Smiling with pride, Legacy took her place onstage. Ink began to narrate from the story she'd written.

"Once upon a time," Ink said, "there was a great tennis champion. Her name was Legacy Petrin, and she knew how to shine in the darkness."

KOBE BRYANT is an Academy Award winner, a *New York Times* best-selling author, and the CEO of Granity Studios, a multimedia content creation company. He spends every day focused on creating stories that inspire the next generation of athletes to be the best versions of themselves. In a previous life, Kobe was a five-time NBA champion, two-time NBA Finals MVP, NBA MVP, and two-time Olympic gold medalist. He hopes to share what he's learned with young athletes around the world.

ANNIE MATTHEW is a novelist and a poet. In a former life, she was a professional athlete. She now lives in Iowa with her gray furry dog, Gus.

GRANITY STUDIOS, LLC

GRANITYSTUDIOS.COM

Library of Congress Control Number: 2019936475
ISBN (hardcover): 9781949520033
ISBN (eBook): 9781949520040

Printed in the United States of America
1 3 5 7 9 10 8 6 4 2

Book design by Karina Granda
Cover design and art direction by Spandana Myneni and Jeff Toye
Calligraphy and title lettering by Seb Lester
Interior art by Ryan Woodward
Endpaper art by Rovina Cai